The Contemptuary

The Contemptuary

David Foster

PUNCHER & WATTMANN

First published in 2018

Published by Puncher and Wattmann
PO Box 441
Glebe NSW 2037

http://www.puncherandwattmann.com

puncherandwattmann@bigpond.com

National Library of Australia
Cataloguing-in-Publication entry:

Foster, David

The Contemptuary

ISBN   9781925780031

I. Title.

A821.3

Cover design by Miranda Douglas. Cover image: 'Clog-an-uudhachta, the Bell of the Will', an ancient Irish monastic hand bell on display in the National Museum of Ireland.

This project has been assisted by the Australian Government through the Australia Council, its arts funding and advisory body.

Australian Government

*We turn more readily to God as our inward witness
when men despise us and think no good of us.*

Thomas a Kempis

Jesus is closer to us when we suffer. He needs victims.

Padre Pio

Author's Note:

The novel is a mix of plausible and factual, a piece of fake news.

The events recounted hereinafter are largely the product of imagination.

The settings however are actual locations.

The principal characters are fictitious. Certain of these fictitious characters will share attributes with real-life individuals but identification of these real-life individuals is a challenge to be resisted. We need to reconfigure the real to confect the unreal that is more-than-real. There was no earthquake in Judaea when the veil of the temple was rent in the midst.

Gerda Foster, Loretta Corrigan, Petrus Boekel and Paddy Murray all provided input in one form or another while I too have done time in Wallyworld.

Take a sip

They held an open day at the gaol December last that families of staff members might gain a more sympathetic understanding of the working environment their oft-times testy loved ones must endure, of why they so frequently ring in sick whenever there's a full moon and of why they habitually brace the back door with a foot as they unlock it. Hasn't been done in decades and I think it a great idea, credit to management as it does entail organization, even a bit of risk. I shouldn't have done it were I the Senior Assistant Super I was due to become. My youngest daughter Fee, Fiona, who works in the Circle as Screener SAPO, Services and Programs Officer responsible for screening inmates on admission, asked did I want to come along as she was taking Olwyn and Constance, but I said no, not my monkeys, not my circus. Access was via the vehicle gate around four p.m. with one poor girl in the gatehouse, which is electronic, but one door won't open till a certain interval after another has shut and you need to pass through several doors, incoming and outgoing. A chaplain goes through twelve doors and gates en route to chapel. It would take our Reverend Ruth twenty minutes to get onto the street. There are no little cafes near the Correctional Complex. Quite a show apparently; there was the scumbag armamentarium, our display of confiscated improvised weaponry in the gatehouse, you could see the visitors' centre where smiles come in in the hairy handbag. Most folk have the idea from watching Foxtel movies that prisoners interact with their visitors through a perspex screen, a box visit. No. While we do have box visits most of our visits are contact and prisoners intermingle with visitors. Dogs can't sniff out all hairy handbags and strictly speaking we have no authority to strip a woman and make her squat and cough but the threat of a box visit would often bring compliance. That said, female officers baulk at stripping black-clad grannies and fossicking soiled nappies and so we get shrooms and xannies and pink rocks and hash and cell phones in the wings and batteries and chargers. Whilst old lags who would never touch a needle get off their faces on moonshine, brewed from Vegemite, telephone disso, Brasso and aftershave and hidden in laundry detergent bottles, half the population injects using syringes, barrels and picks modified to fit inside the hairy handbag. The salubrious maxim 'clean fit each hit no shit' falls by the wayside as inmates share fits with blunt picks. They share tattoo guns fashioned from cassette machine motors and textile shop sewing machine needles using ink made from art class charcoal. Chasers become facultative blasters, given the penalty for a dirty urine; loss of visits, buy-ups, telephone calls, your current classo, is applied irrespective of drug. Boys in blue would prefer all scumbags off their tits on bush buds but the piss-persistent if innocuous cone announces its ignition and so half the prison population has STIs and BBVs, mostly hep C. A few are HIV plus. A good few are in because of dealing and/or clumsy armed robs. The chilly city thus stands in the front-line of Nixon's War against Drugs.

There is also a widespread notion we would have a communal mess hall, a commensality where plots are hatched, no: Goulburn inmates chow down in their cells. At open day there were no convicts on display but you could peruse industries, woodwork, the textile shop, though not the distal X-wing demounts, the concrete tennis court, the soothing views of the timbered Cookbundoon range as seen from the oval, the dog squad gave a display by the gym with lots of canine leaps, there was a sausage sizzle, the kids were free to clamber in and out of a meat wagon, but what impressed both Fee and me, was they opened up the wings; not X-wing or the MPU, 'the Boneyard' as it houses 'dogs', argot for informers, or HRMCC, separate gaols, but Fee said you could walk from office to office the entire bottom landing of the four old wings, built the year they hanged Ned Kelly, that radiate out from the Circle, the roofs of which can be seen over the razor wire and twenty-foot high walls, in the middle distance, across the General Cemetery from Sydney Road, Marys Mount as backdrop. Would you like fries with that? Visitors weren't free to climb the steps to the upper landings, two in the case of B and C-wing, one in the case of A and D, but look at the ground floor shower block. Forget that cake of soap, an empty cell awaits. Thirteen by seven, nine-foot-six high with a small barred window that only a man nine-foot-three high can see through, in you go now *gotcha*! Imagine the three-quarter-inch iron door, fitted with what in 1880 was the latest in bolts and keepers, slammed shut and secured with an old brass Jackson lock from Lonnie. Two beds to each slot. Are you sharing your slot with a gronk? That is the fate a recidivist most fears, a gronk being a moron, not to be confused with a 'chat', who seldom showers and farts and burps and snores and picks his nose. You couldn't see or hear them but you knew that they were there as you could read their tags with their names and yards; Leb yard, Koori yard, Aussie

Islander, Aussie Asian. Putting a man in a wrong yard is a screw's worst fear. Each yard accommodates thirty inmates constituting a scumbag platoon. The wing in contrast is company size. Fee says there was lots of shouting initially from upper tiers, enough to impress the girls, and the usual barrage of toilet paper that celebrates any lockdown was finding its way through the bars into the yards. I asked Constance, who's just turned five, what most impressed her and she said 'the toilets.'

Oh they're good for a smile, the little girls not the toilets. I love the way during baptisms, mostly done two at a time at Sunday's choral Eucharist, how to celebrate one of the three occasions she'll see the inside of a church — water on the head, be-wed then dead — a little heathen three-timer will do a twirl in the aisle of the nave as we vastly outnumbered regulars, cranky from kneeling at unfamiliar stations, prepare to applaud what we suspect to be perjury from the chancel. But we have to give you the benefit of the doubt in the Cathedral Church.

Not so in the slammer. I recall a sergeant-at-arms of an outlaw motorcycle gang and I can tell you which one as we have the tatts of each known gang on a chart in reception, who walking in my close company to the Circle to get his yawns (you get your pills and your methadone swill from the clinic sister in the Circle, which is the donjon, began working life as a chapel, as it says itself in MCCMXXCIII, and has on its roof a disused belltower of the same vintage as the disused belltower on Marys Mount, as well as your DXXVIII pre-release dollars from Centrelink) roared across at the rockies' yard 'You love *fuckin* kids ya cunts but we fuckin *love* kids!'

He was always there or thereabouts, our Zoltan. Patched members of motorcycle gangs hold rockies (paedophiles) in particular odium while bikie defectors, being known to know too much, are the dogs most at risk. Bikies will always have an old lady and a few kids outside and whilst in boob will often send these kids to exclusive private schools. Imagine the horror on learning from watching Nine Network News that Knox and Trinity Grammar and St Ignatius harbour rock spiders and yes we have free-to-air TV if we've been good boys.

A lad in the MPU listens to ABC Jazz. Just listens to channel 201 while reading the Periodic Table. He writes some interesting poetry too and quite popular. Let's see if I recall the one a friend of mine found by the G-block photocopier;

2-CD PCP alpha-methyltryptamine
LSZee DOC foxymethoxy mephedrone
3-mmc phenmetrazine
4-fluoromethamphetamine
Flephedrone methaqualone
Pemoline methiopropamine

That's the first verse of several but you get the gist. The Eighth Century Rule
of Ailbe was also written metrically. That was to assist the Old Irish monks in
memorizing the Old Irish. Rhythm and rhyme are mnemonic devices.

Old bikies, and we're not talking Leb yard Nike bikies, have cast-iron ethics. The
Hells Angels were established by demobbed veterans from World War Two even
as certain of their peers took the strait gate and entered religious orders. All
were used to uniformed hardship and rigid military discipline. A Russian sniper
who later became an Orthodox archimandrite saw off more German soldiers
during the battle for Stalingrad than were killed by the entire French army during the whole of World War Two. Such men were accustomed to pulling together
against a common foe. When Comancheros who survived the Milperra Massacre
did boob at Long Bay MRC, Jock, Chewy and Sunshine had them all painting
Twelve-wing. That's dead-set painting Twelve-wing not just sweeping Twelve-
wing. Goulburn is presently the Rebels' gaol; Bandidos go to Parklea. We can't
have certain inmates in the same gaol.

    The present Anglican chaplain is assistant priest in the Cathedral. Chapel
today is in G-block, education block. When I was a baggy we didn't have a chapel
and rainmakers had to meet up with their clients in the cells, while services were
held in the wings, directly over the main offices, in little rooms that aren't used
anymore for security reasons.

    One of them has a carpet-covered trapdoor in the floor and how the gigs love
to see it, happen the carpet be folded back.

    'Gigs' are outsiders visiting a gaol purely for perving purposes, while as to
these clients, keep an open mind: Samoans use a condom machine as a hair gel
dispenser while I know a man who took a leak behind a tree at a picnic and,

spotted by a stone butch, found himself in court defending a charge of indecent exposure. He's now on the sex offenders' register.

Toilets! Let's talk toilets, let's have some dirty toilet talk. One to each slot, a few to each yard, irrefrangible stainless steel since the Abo emeute of ten years back destroyed D-wing, the two-story D-wing in which inmates are now mostly on remand, yet to face a court.

No toilet seats and no toilet lids to the toilets, naked toilets. Stark in the slots, which are less a double en suite with twin singles than a big dunny, a big dunny with two beds because the toilet is the gazingstock. It glistens. It can be seen from the door. Yes, there is a steel hand basin as well, but the toilet is the gazingstock. No screen to provide privacy so you void your bowel in full view of the gronk and whoever is peeking through the judas hole and the gronk will void his bowel in full earshot of you, a look-at-me, listen-to-me loo, the design world's 2015 gig-inspired fancy anticipated. In the yards the handful of cans in each latrine is the only yard feature though each yard has a few benches and tables, ultra-sturdy. There is a screen but it's only a screen of a sort, a half-mask if you like. You can still see the cans because if you're a screw, you need to see what's going on around the cans.

So when you're inside you live in a dunny, you eat in a dunny, you sleep in a dunny and you share your dunny, for the most part, with a stranger who also lives in the dunny. That's to remind you that you're a piece of shit and what's more, a bigger piece of shit than most. When Pico della Mirandola coined the phrase 'the dignity of man' in the fifteenth century, he must have forgotten that he had an arsehole and he hadn't completed his gender studies course. There is no dignity in being a creature that shits, Pico, end of story. Man was not made in God's image because God does not have an arsehole. God has only a cakehole. God has dignity because He is a spirit as Christ tells us, and spirits don't shit.

Toilet paper! Where would we be without toilet paper in Corrections? Just the thing to hurl into the yard to valorise your grievances but there is another use to which a two-ply toilet roll may be put, and I don't mean wiping an arse, though sagacious care of the arsehole is to be recommended in a setting where your arsehole is your most valuable negotiable security. Hanging out for a whack of hammer? Know how you can score a cap without having to pay cash? Just let someone fuck you without using a condom. Blasting ice but can't find a vein? Douche with the tipless barrel (think safety, use lube). Scored a whack on your contact though you're wearing overalls with 'visits' printed on them, zips secured with cable ties, don't want to lose it on the strip search? You will be asked to squat and spread but well you know where you can safely hide a cut-down thirty-mill fit.

> God the Father is shown with a bum
> In the Sistine Chapel in Rome
> Because he was made in the image of man
> It stands to reason he would have a bum
> But Michelangelo must have been first
> To sneak behind him and glimpse it
> Why on earth would God have a bum?
> Purely in order to sit on his throne
> There being no toilets in Heaven
> But are there toilets in Hell perhaps?
> There are and no toilet brushes
> A loo for each two cellar dwellers at least
> Mind you Satan (whom Allah accurse!)
> Has hooves and horns as we know
> Which means he's vegetarian
> So the smell's not too bad there below

Collect for purity

We all have a tale to tell if we can be arsed to tell it. We all have a tale we mustn't tell, we all have a tale we need to tell. The tale we mustn't tell, we mustn't tell lest it wound or traduce others who all have their own reminiscences. The tale we need to tell is the tale we mustn't tell.

If we have none to whom to speak, we will tell the tale to ourselves. To whom do we speak when we speak to ourselves? The one who speaks is not the one who listens.

May the one who listens be the one to whom all hearts are open, from whom no secrets are hidden and to whom all desires are known.

A man who is pure in soul and without sin in his mode of life always speaks the words of the Spirit with chastity and he judges both the Divine and what is in himself in accordance with the measure of his understanding. But if a man's heart is filled with passions, these passions move also his tongue. Even if he speaks of spiritual matters, he does so under the influence of passions. A wise man notices such a one at the first meeting and a pure man smells his stench
St Isaac of Nineveh

> Dudley Leahy walked all the way from Uluru to Windsor
> Pushing a trolley from IGA to raise money for cancer
> He sent it to an institute the other side of Canberra
> That spent the money then said to Dudley, we still don't know the answer
> Bottle of steam and a bit of skirt
> Two might kill you but one won't hurt

Trevi Fountain here I come

Zounds: *Elizabethan expletive, abbreviation of 'by God's wounds', in reference to the topical wounds doubted by Doubting Thomas, borne by the Christ as a result of crucifixion on Calvary.*

Zounds! Can't breathe. But now I'm sitting up in a bed so it was a dream. Methought me under a scrum collapse and couldn't breathe but now I'm sitting up on a mattress, don't know where I am. You know the feeling, you wake in a strange bed don't know where you are. I'm sitting on the side of a bed and it's not my bed at Willochra. I can hear a couple of plovers making a racket somewhere nearby. They are probably outside the gaol in the old St Saviour's Cemetery.

Ah yes. Then it comes to me. I am in a cell. I have been locked into an A-wing slot, fully clothed with no pyjamas on. I am long gone like a turkey through the corn, long gone with my long pyjamas on. No.

In the absence of fire or riot there's not a lot to do between lock-in and let-go, but three of us were on that night, my first night in Goulburn Gaol following orientation day, my first night on the job. A roster clerk had seen to it. Those were the days. As a baggy, I was there to do as I was told, but also present doing bugger-all was PO One Macintosh, a waddling echidna who'd had to apply to become a two-striper, whereas I got my second stripe as a matter of course after four years. AS in charge of A-wing that night was Laid-Back Lester, always to be found to be in his office seat, feet on desk, reading a form guide. The two seemed less than pleased to see me, even a little surprised. Indeed Lester sent Tosh to check the roster board in the gatehouse.

Shortly after lock-in Assistant Superintendent Lester took me to a cell, unlocked it, satisfied himself it was still empty and ordered me in. This will do you the world of good, he'd said as he'd shut the door. Grab some shut-eye. It is a tradition in this gaol that every baggy must spend his first night in a slot, the better to understand what he is dealing with (yeah right, try telling that to a spinner). I later learned that no one ever heard of this 'tradition', but as I was a baggy, albeit a baggy of forty-two which is a pretty hairy-arsed baggy, I did as I was told till after twelve months on probation I finally received my first stripe, which came as a relief because when inmates see a baggy they will always try on a con.

I sat on the bed going over the dream.

At five a.m. Tosh unlocked the door saying 'Wakey wakey hands off snakey, I need you to lend an assust.' There was no panic to his Kiwi voice. I followed him as we went to a slot in the Circle end of the upper landing and as we climbed the stairs I glanced at the office where the case files are kept, and I could see Laid-Back Lester in his seat, feet on desk, reading a form guide.

An open cell had the door on-the-bolt. There was a strong smell of shit. Sitting in this shit, purple in the face with a noose around his neck, was an ithyphallic man. He was barefoot and stark naked. He had shat himself severely. He had barely a whisk of pubic hair but the hair on his head was silver-white, platinum-blond like Max von Sydow's. He had shit in his hair.

'Take the weight' said Tosh 'while I go get the nine uluven.' Well no he wouldn't have said that as we didn't call them nine elevens before nine eleven, but we still had our nine eleven, which is a small twisted cutting implement that cannot be used to slash or stab but is excellent for sharpening pencils, two of which are kept in each wing for the express purpose of cutting through ligatures generally made from pyjama tops.

'Do we have any gloves?' I asked.

No. Help yourself to Hep A. As Tosh strolled off, whistling as he went, to find the nine eleven, I supported the inmate's torso to take the weight off the ligature. He was slumped forward, sitting in his shit between the toilet and the sink, facing the toilet. The noose was attached to the tap in the sink and went from the inmate's neck to his wrists, which he'd lashed together at the groin, and on to his genitals, behind the balls, to function as a kind of cock ring. He was covered in wounds.

Fuck, I thought, how good is this? To make matters worse, nothing was being done in accordance with the DIC check list. In the first place, FRO, First Responding Officer, should have been Laid-Back Lester, because for any cell to be opened between the hours of lock-in and let-go requires, for security purposes, the presence of the OIC. Yet here was I, a green baggy, being left alone in a situation that demanded the prompt attention of Justice Health, or if none of their personnel was on duty, and they probably weren't at that hour, the Goulburn zambucks.

While I supported the inmate's armpits I found myself staring, not so much at his tackle, the way the little girls in their prams in the men's change rooms always do before they stare you square in the eye, but at his hands and feet, as these were somewhat in my face and had lesions the size of a dilated arsehole, one to each foot about the second metatarsal, and back of each hand about the middle metacarpal. Strange looking wounds: in colour they were reddish-black and, as I have sworn on a Good Book to a table of men in black habits, they weren't bleeding. They were slightly scabbed, somewhat black, symmetrical and clearly deep, but were they healing? This was the question. Did they appear to be healing? They were certainly disappearing, indeed they disappeared as I watched and were naught but rubicund splotches by the time a wheezing Tosh returned with the nine eleven. Were they free from swelling and suppuration? Were they pleasantly scented? Did there appear to be inflammation about the surrounding tissue? The Congregation Superior-General asked me this over and again at my Passionist interrogation, which took place at Passionist Headquarters, Piazza SS. Giovanni e Paolo, close by the Colosseum, as I was to receive in the mail, much to my surprise and delight, a return business-class airfare to Rome in May of 1990, an invitation extended me, I think we may safely assume, as the result of a confidence I'd shared with the Catholic chaplain at the time, a certain Sister Edmund. I'd mentioned to Sister Edmund I'd seen something in the main street of Katoomba that hit me like a fend from Eddy Pettybourne, but we'll get back to that, Inshallah. Suffice it to say that neither autopsy nor subsequent coronial inquest made any mention of scarification or wounds to the hands and feet, or so I was assured by the men in black. I couldn't locate the documentation. I must assume the zambucks noted nothing untoward and as Tosh had returned to the wilds of Aotearoa within a month of the incident, I was sole witness. As to a transverse lesion in the region of the fifth to ninth ribs, I hadn't looked at the inmate's ribs. But when I took a closer look at the noose around his neck, I saw it was made of toilet paper — toilet paper, rolled lengthwise into half-metre strips then pleached into three strands.

Where there's a will there's a noose.

Do not hurl that toilet roll into the vast blue yonder
Wipe your arse or neck yourself the choice is yours to ponder
But should you choose to neck yourself, to foil the First Responder
Who'll earn a commendation should he thwart your anaconda
Just eat up big distend your bowel
And offer him a chore from hell

A who's who of blue

After a spell at uni in the cold reign of Bob Ellis, and having returned to Grabby where I tried and failed to make the farm a goer, I found myself once more in Sydney, this time way out Matraville way, doing such silly things as entering a disused, teargas-filled tower, there to remove a gas mask and utter my name and rank.

Dudley Leahy cough choke, probationary cough choke officer.

Oh how they laughed.

It was Bill informed me of Mumbles' impending funeral, old Bill, canon residentiary, retired chalkie much given to quoting from poets like William Cowper in his sermons; that'll bring the young folk in, Bill, though it makes a pleasant change from C.S. Lewis and W.H. Auden. Somehow, Bill had learned I was in the gaol when Mumbles was governor. I don't drink at the Gordon or the Workers Club so don't keep in touch. Don't read the Goulburn Penny Post. Bill sings in our miserable excuse for a choir when not required to celebrate, and he only preaches if the sub-dean's ill or the dean attending a synod. Our choir may well be the world's worst, but our organ, famously, is one of the best, a splendid Forster and Andrews from 1884, and from a tonal perspective, the Hull-based firm (Hull is other people? Larkin?) was producing its finest instruments between 1870 and 1900. Our building's architect, Edmund Blacket, had a say in the design of the organ. He was hands on, our Edmund; hand carved, as a piece of scrimshaw, the crucifix that hangs over the pulpit.

The voicing and finishing of our organ ensures we attract the best players, and we recently enjoyed Martin Rein's rendition of Marcel Dupré's Variations sur un Noël, with Martin's wooden dummy work on flute stops between each variation well-nigh Jackie Chan speed. The postlude, or concluding voluntary, is the consolation of the choral Eucharist, as we may expect the likes of Henri Mulet's Carillon Sortie, or J.S. Bach's Toccata and Fugue in D Minor. Blame it on the organ I'm Anglican, though I do admire sandstone, and St Saviour's Cathedral Church is white Bundanoon sandstone. In contrast, SS. Peter and Paul down the road, our ex-Catholic Cathedral, is Bungonia greenstone and only has a W. Hill organ. That said, it has the Murphy bell.

Bill needs a hip job for mine; he finds it a struggle to ascend the pulpit. His mic, egged on by a daemon in his trousers pocket, is prone to feed back. He does the service at St Stephan's Pejar if it's the fifth Sunday in the month and returns the collection tied in the corner of a two-tone blue handkerchief. As in the manner of Javier Bardem in *No Country for Old Men* he came limping down the aisle on the Seventh Sunday after Pentecost, veering toward the pew it appears he knows I arrogate, without so much as glancing towards me he side-valved 'See me after the service Dud.'

Always one to avoid me in the greeting of peace, the canon. Never once have I felt the strength of the man's hand. He just shakes hands with the verger then, from the choir stalls, gives our picayune congregation a generalised wave of benediction.

It would have been the assistant priest alerted Bill to the funeral, but she wasn't present on the Seventh Sunday after Pentecost. Nor did she process in the procession of Stephen Saint and Martyr the following week. Always makes a beeline for me in the greeting of peace though, bless her, and still pulling in that much-needed sixty-seven grand a year paid direct to the diocese. It is she serves as full-time Anglican chaplain at what is at present four gaols, though it has been one and on occasion two. While formerly a place of dark cells and hardwood gags to which the government flogger was still paying visits from Darlinghurst, it today consists in the High Risk Management Correctional Centre, HRMCC, SuperMax; A-wing and the MPU or Multi-Purpose Unit (segro, protection and strict one-out protection); the low-security X-wing and the maximum-security main: four gaols housed within one inexpugnable complex of six wings with twelve yards housing five-hundred-plus malefactors.

Visiting some miscreant for the first time and don't know which way to turn? Then don't bother looking for a street sign pointing to 'Correctional Complex' because there isn't one and it can't be because we're ashamed of the place when it employs half the district. Reverend Ruth, at present on her annual recycling scrounge for spent Christmas cards, will have done the three-day security awareness course, and the five-day orientation, and the pastoral education course, all run by the CCAC, but I'd be surprised if too many lads feel commoved to consult her. Her main challenge would have been finding someone to explain the computer.

There is one scumbag in for the duration when all he'd wanted was a few smiles, to which as a registered nurse he'd been helping himself. As to the fire he set, which put a few oxygen thieves out of misery, the devil made him do it, or so he told the rozzers. And he's Anglican.

Isn't it a shocking thing entirely when the former VC of a university can set fire to a nursing home?

It's a Messy church, our Anglican Church. One glimpse of the deeply uncharismatic Archbishop of Canterbury tells you that. No Thomas à Becket our Most Reverend and Right Honourable Justin Welby. Beckett led an army through Poitiers.

'Honour Guard' says your man in the Sam Browne belt, swagger stick a-tuck, 'Slow March!' And six screws in navy blue, including a bull dyke and a Filipino, wearing white gloves and black left plastic shoulder bands, march from the car park. They march to the beat of the NSW Department of Corrective Services Band, as represented by a bass drum muffled to produce a lifeless thump, and two snare drums, snares released to create the field drum timbre. A solitary bugler brings up the rear in front of the shiny black Sidney Craig hearse. The bugler is there to sound the Last Post as the coffin retreats behind the curtain. CS bandsmen, despite the uniform, are not as they once were serving prison officers, but rather musos, riff-raff employed at a casual rate of thirty bucks an hour, and will make no attempt to fraternise with such officers as find they cannot fit into the Gothic chapel. Well, it was a chapel once: you can still see the stump of what was a sandstone cross on the ridge over the gable, hasn't even been angle-ground off square. During the service the drummers seek the shelter of the Cypress pines behind the columbarium. If they'd contemplated a furtive smoke they decide against it. I'd swear as to short-sleeved shirts; as to the kilts, I may have watched too many Bundanoons as Brigadoon, and caution; like Canberra's Floriade, if you've seen it once, you've seen it.

Goulburn was once renowned for music. Our fifteen-piece all-inmate orchestra under the baton of a lifer was a regular feature on radio 2SM during the forties.

Eleven a.m.; the gaol would have been in lockdown had there not been training the previous day, but even so, fifty or sixty two- and three-stripers are present, and many retirees, some in suits, most in leather jackets, though I wore my cream Fair Isle sweater. In a life lagging, twenty-odd years, I made it to Assistant Super, a one-pipper that put me in charge of a wing, but I keep to myself. I never had much to say and I always drink alone, so I made myself unmemorable and that way I survive. Mind you I was forty-two when I became a baggy, 14 July '86, and the herrenvolk didn't at first like the cut of my jib, though I'd played tighthead for the Dirty Reds and before that Sydney Uni and my family is well known round Grabby. Took a year before they'd let me hold a set of keys.

Also present in civvies I see many long-term non-custodial staff, most of whom had a soft spot for Mumbles. What would have been, in his day and mine, Welfare and A and OD workers, nowadays designated SAPO's and Senior SAPO's and Psyches and MOSPs, and of course today we have a general manager rather than a governor. By the door, receiving commiseration, the family of the deceased and greeting all as they enter, Ron Woodham, only baggy ever made it through to commish. Ron Woodham, forty-six years in the service, retired in 2012 but still serving on the Parole Board. Ron Woodham, who told the Prisons Minister in 2005 'My job is to watch your back. My job is to ensure that, as you step down, you will be bruised and not battered.'

That same minister (Hatzistergos) remarked on vacating the portfolio, '*Anyone* could run Corrective Services with Ron Woodham in charge.'

Too true. Say what you will of Ron he took the job seriously. He could recite to you chapter and verse the form of every one of the ten-thousand-odd scumbags housed in the state's twenty-eight gaols. He was famous for it. He knew Who was Who in the Zoo.

We heard how Mumbles became a baggy three years after Ron, in '68. That was the year our A-wing decedent, July '86, was ordained priest. Though the service was conspicuously secular, a counsellor from the Apostolic Nunciature in Canberra read a message from the Concilium Legionis Mariae, from which we learned Mumbles had been a member of the Dublin-based Legion of Mary, and had done good work for the Legion, though the nature of the work was not specified.

Craig Funerals, who own the hearse and run the Craig's Hill Crematorium, have a couple of speakers set up outside the now-deconsecrated chapel, but the amp isn't properly working so we can't hear all that's said. We hear enough.

We hear the music, selected by Mumbles who died of cancer in the Canberra Hospice; Jailhouse Rock for the note of manly levity, It's a Wonderful World to bring a tear to the eye, Knockin' on Heaven's Door from Guns and Roses. I stood apart among the headstones of the Catholic religious who are buried there in their hundreds. I'd never before been to the place, didn't know it existed. You drive past the gaol towards Tarlo and turn left at the hostelry of Patrick Confoy.

A few one-pippers are glancing my way invitingly but I ignore them. They didn't have to vote me off the island, friends; I took a powder. Perhaps they imagine I'm a former inmate planning a disturbance. Built like Brad Thorn, Mumbles; six-foot-six, nineteen stone and a bit of a short fuse. Give an Islander Yard gaffer pause, the prospect of a blue with Mumbles. Mumbles began working life, as we heard from Ron, as a mechanic in Barry. No little Australian boy dreams of becoming a screw. Some of us are former jumbo pilots, some master mariners, some butchers, some graziers, all lured by the prospect of steady pay for doing bugger-all with untold overtime. In the early noughties you could pull a six-figure annual wage at Long Bay.

Whereas today, when they lock down X-wing, they leave it unattended overnight.

In his final posting Mumbles departed to become a desk jockey, assistant commish, while I stayed on until the DIC witnessed on my first night overwhelmed me. It took a while.

It may have been suspected I was a dog breeder. In his retirement Mumbles devoted himself to the breeding of dogs, and we heard from Ron how he wouldn't just sell a dog to anyone: you had to satisfy him that you were a fit and proper person to own a dog. A young female two-striper had a Neapolitan mastiff on a short leash, which in due course entered the ex-chapel to pay its last respects to its breeder.

I got on well with Mumbles. We shared some hard times but we also shared a liking for the phrase 'these cuffs are too tight'. Back in the late eighties before CCTV, we had twenty-five deaths — murders, suicides, ODs — within the space of two years, and you should see the paperwork for any Death in Custody. It is big.

To cite one instance; a young man, who'd OD'd on 'done and benzos, acquiring his benzos presumably via the hairy handbag, wasn't on the MMT. So someone who was had regurgitated methadone syrup in payment of a favour and does it taste foul, but off the 'done, out of gaol, back to using, back to gaol: the well-worn path. Mumbles didn't leave the district when he retired as governors usually do. A former inmate of my acquaintance was astounded to encounter him in a Woolworths' aisle. 'Hello Mr Sheehan' says the ex-inmate. 'Call me Mumbles,' mumbles Mumbles.

Son of Man can these ashes arise, can these ashes live again?
Then prophesy upon these ashes and say, O ye dry ashes when
Ye took a turn in the cinerary urn, Hold on says Ezekiel
Thy Word has not been heard since fire pulverized the bone
So when the last trump sounds I fear
Nary a cupboard door may stir

Alligator pair

I often drive to Canberra on Sunday after Mass as it's an easy drive from Goulburn, and scenic too, if you like Hereford cattle and Lombardy poplar. I can drive home through Stunnedaroo and Stunning. I wouldn't want to live in Canberra: a warder has to knock on your door at Alexander Maconochie, that's the prison they named after the Norfolk Island Gaoler. If too drunk to drive, I will check myself into University House to rest my paws on the butterbox joints of a Fred Ward wingback easy chair that would have been fashioned of Blackwood by one of Jennings' Germans, though many of Jennings' Germans were actually Dutch resistance. Putting the past as best they could behind in 1950, Jennings' Germans ventured to a Canberra then the size of Goulburn, to hypostatise for Fred his unique, bespoke furniture that confers the comfy Modernist ambiance on the ANU. My father rather fancied himself a frustrated cabinetmaker and took me as a boy on many a visit to old Acton. We would sneak abashed in and out of various buildings.

Weather being fine, I may cycle or stroll round the lake, which takes a couple of hours by cycle if you ride out through the Jerrabomberra Wetlands. I acknowledge a *frisson* to see a gowned man sitting in the garden of the hospice. I search his face for signs.

In the case of rain, I might browse in the National Library, depress myself. Once in a while I used to take in a film at the Arc Cinema, pretty much out of action these days owing to budgetary constraints, which is a shame, although the Sunday viewers, myself included, were mostly flashing a concession card. The Cinema, which is in the National Film and Sound Archive building, used to be the Institute of Anatomy, had Phar Lap's heart on display, is a fine example of Monaro Art Deco, and ran in its final season a selection of Ingmar Bergman films, most of them new thirty-five millimetre prints courtesy of the Swedish Film Institute, that focussed on the relationship between Bergman and Norwegian actress Liv Ullmann, one of the many actresses with whom he'd enjoyed a tread albeit his main muse. I viewed the entire season, because I recall seeing *Wild Strawberries* and *The Virgin Spring* at the Savoy in Bligh Street when I was new to Sydney during my undergraduate days. It was the only venue in Sydney screened non-English foreign films. I saw the paedophile Roman Polanski's debut at the Savoy. You could buy a coffee in the foyer as well, it was the acme of sophistication. It closed in the early seventies along with the old Adyar Bookshop that stood nearby.

'We all want to fuck young girls,' observed Polanski in his own defence. He was using the word broadly: he sodomised her as well, having first drugged her.

I'm pretty sure it was in a Bergman film I first heard anyone speak in a non-Latin foreign tongue. To this day I delight in the intonation of the Swedish tongue on the rare occasions I hear it.

I once had a Swedish mule in my wing who'd never set eyes on the Wide Brown Land. He had to conjure it up from what he could hear beyond the wall. Arrested at the airport, taken straight to Goulburn.

How comforting to hear again the Swedish tongue and to see once more those vivid, wind-swept pines on the Baltic isle upon which Bergman shot so many of his seminal black and white features, and how very slow-moving those features seem today. It was on the stony beach in front of Bergman's Faro farmhouse that the knight, played by a typically grim and gaunt Max von Sydow, had his fateful game of chess. Walking back to my vehicle having just watched *Saraband*, shot in 2003, Bergman's final film as director starring Liv Ullmann at sixty-five, the older the fiddle the sweeter the tune, I realised for the first time that the impact Bergman's films had upon me as a teenage virgin was largely attributable to the close-ups of the face of Liv Ullmann. Why, even now in my seventies, I could recognise every freckle as she faced off against Max von Sydow in *Shame*, filmed in '68. I wonder to what extent other cinephile ephebes may have imprinted on Ullmann, thanks to Bergman, as the archetype of feminine allure. Sven Nykvist, his cinematographer, prefers natural light, which doesn't amount to much in those hyperborean latitudes, and focusses heavily, in every film he shoots, on facial expression, notably those of Bergman's paramours, Liv, Harriet, Bibi et al. And we now know what we merely suspected back in the mid-sixties, that the human being sees a human face through dedicated facial-recognition software, quite distinct from other components of the visual optics. A face is not an arse, whence I guess the proscription on doggy sex in the Holy Kabbala. In his screenplays Bergman flaunts his 'Stradivarius', which is what he called her, she tells us so herself, and seeing again at the Arc such a paean to Ullmann as *Persona*, I recall how I felt with my face so close to hers when she would have been in her twenties. I recall my awe at what I should have deemed our unaccountable proximity, as well as the deference I would have shown any man who seemed to interest her, which in those days was Bergman, with whom at the time she was brawling in the aforementioned Faro farmhouse off the Gotland coast. In Dheeraj Akolkar's 2013 documentary, *Liv and Ingmar: Painfully Connected*, Ullmann at seventy-five complains with a smile of what a recluse he was, what a terrible temper he had, how he wouldn't let her off the isle to socialise. I noted in *Faithless*, 2000, directed in the style of Bergman by Ullmann but scripted by Bergman, that the octogenarian Bergman has Erland Josephson, cast as "the theatre director called 'Bergman'" attention Norwegian novelist Karl Ove Knausgaard, explaining a condition he calls, apologetically, 'retrospective jealousy' which is likewise alluded to in *Scenes from a Marriage*, 1973.

So there clearly existed a problem, yet sexual love, as the young intuit, extends beyond one life. It pre-exists and survives us. Only because of this could we enter so willingly the servitude of marriage. The one with whom we fall in love is intriguingly familiar and fixed at the age of first sighting: he never loved who loved not at first sighting. Sex is a beastly business thus bestowing the beast's eternal present, so that there could be no such torment as retrospective jealousy. There is only jealousy.

In the year after the screening of *Scenes from a Marriage* on Swedish TV the divorce rate in Sweden increased fifty percent.

None, incidentally, was ever 'retrospectively' jealous of a legally married spouse as he had no choice but to take the bad with the good. Bergman was twenty years older than Ullmann when she left her (psychiatrist) husband for him; a very successful ladies' man, the theatre director called Bergman. Long life and large progeny, unusual in world history. Married five times and fathered nine children, including one with Ullmann whom he never married, but by age eighty-five he'd begun to rue the cost of the Sexual Revolution, which more or less began in Sweden and probably with him. A bit of a pandar in the working of his cinematic spell, the sexual magus, but all these sightings of Max von Sydow drew my mind to the platinum-blond decedent, because Mumbles' funeral was held on the Tuesday after the Ullmann-cum-Bergmanfest concluded with *Cries and Whispers*, 1972, and when Jesus meets his mother at the Fourth Station of the Cross, which stood in the nineteen-sixties in the garden of the Presentation Retreat, she is portrayed as pretty much the same age as Jesus.

Her mandatory fecundity.

Bergman was still making movies long into the age of the digital edit; that said, Donald Fagen still writes songs that appeal to me and I would argue for *Gaucho* as the last great analogue studio production.

Apologies for the stench but I am rather dirty at present, even a bit on the nose with kin, as it seems I took a turn outside Jim Murphy's Airport Cellars and certain of my daughters are keen to cite it as evidence that I can no longer care for myself on the farm, which is bullshit. Oh yes, I forget how to open the car door and found myself fumbling with the fast glass switches, but that could happen to anyone.

> Some of us wear hearing aids and most of us boast dentures
> We'd never drive our four-wheel drive on four-wheel drive adventures
> And we'd hoped to die in the prime of life before incurring censure
> But we all wound up in this nursing home afflicted with dementia
> And by the bed is a Dixie cup
> And you take a sip and you tough the fuck up

Bergman's Faro farmhouse is preserved as a shrine and remains as it was at the time of the auteur's death. It contains a video library in which the elderly Bergman could sit and watch such films as *Crocodile Dundee*, though maybe he didn't actually watch that film, though he had a copy.

Maybe he couldn't watch all of it.

Toothbrushes their uses

The platinum-blond decedent had something in his hands I'd not noticed, given they were clenched into fists and lashed with the ligature and rigor mortis was setting in. Tosh, who'd been meaning to play golf but would now have to write and submit an incident report before ceasing duty, drew my attention to it as he deployed the nine eleven: it was the end of a sharpened toothbrush, a common prison shiv. Tosh indicated puncture wounds to each of the inmate's thighs which, in contrast to those I'd seen or thought I'd seen, were jagged and bloodied. Making no attempt to resuscitate the man, although required to do so, Tosh began marking out the perimeter using tape from the office. Each DIC must be treated as a crime scene.

'Remps up the buzz. Any pulse?'

'No.'

'Good.'

'What do you mean ramps up the buzz?'

'This is a choke and stroke. A choke and a stroke from a man of the cloth, our Reverend Rocky Buzzacott, wirst of the wirst. Choke and a stroke gone wrong.'

'Why isn't the AS here? Doesn't the OIC have to confirm from the FRO what action has been taken?'

'Sittle down Leddy. All is under control. Duty Off has been informed and is notifying the filth.'

'And the ambulance?'

'Yis. Now did you require counselling?'

I did, but am still waiting as I found myself ordered by Laid-Back Lester to watch another cock in action, this time pissing into a jar. A random is generally done at the hour of Lauds when piss is least dilute. Two male officers, which back then was most, and well I recall my first rencounter with my first female officer, who'd hair like Lola in *Run Lola Run*, and silenced a yard full of outlaw bikies by telling them how she often pushed her husband's bike off its stand, came into the gatehouse saying 'who do I need to fuck to get a coffee round here?' Last we heard of Gillian she was governing Dillwynia — in this case Tosh and me, were to watch the micturition, having first conducted a strip search, then screw a lid on the warm jar and affix a seal in the inmate's view. The details would be written on the seal. The security seal number would be entered on a form and the inmate asked to read both form and sticker and attest the numbers matched but he couldn't produce could he, so he had to be placed in a dry yard for two hours but we didn't have one, so I was consigned to remain in his slot and watch he didn't try to 'flush' i.e. guzzle water, all pretty pointless as rockies are rarely on the gear and seldom subjected to a random. But it got me out the way. And by the time the two hours was up, the body upstairs had been removed — I reckon Lester hadn't even seen it — and I was sent in with mop and bucket to rid the slot of shit and semen. I told them in Rome the man had been a gasper like Michael Hutchence stroke David Carradine but they didn't seem interested. I also thought it strange that no one had bothered to interview me, but when I remarked on this to Tosh he replied 'You are jest a baggy.'

I didn't ask the inmate's name and as Tosh had removed his door tag, it wasn't till I was driving home through Pomeroy it hit me. I had seen that head of hair. I'd seen that man before.

You could never actually count on going home till you made it out the gate.

We had some twenty-five years beforehand given each other a perfunctory nod, but we'd moved in different circles and attended different schools. I'd gone to Goulburn High (Justice and Tenacity) while he'd been at St Pat's (Age Quod Agis). It would have been the year after I left Goulburn we met and all it amounted to was a nod of the head.

Autumn term was Michaelmas term at Sydney Uni in them days and during Easter break I came home to Goulburn on the train. I still had Brenda my Catholic girlfriend, and as all Tykes, which didn't include me or my father, we being lapsed Tykes, ex-Tykes, would faithfully visit the Stations of the Cross, which since 1955 had meant traipsing round the Presentation Retreat, I'd said to the lovely Brenda, with a vulpine cunning, I don't really want to be traipsing round with three thousand people come Friday, but I wouldn't mind seeing these statues that I've heard so much about. See, I figured once I got her into that garden I could paw her about. Medieval Muslim writers allude to the monastery garden with a smirk, suggesting an ancient association with sex and alcohol. Up we went to Marys Mount early that Holy Week, and I recall being mightily delighted to see the garden, as I thought, deserted. Women were debarred from the monastery buildings though not from the monastery garden. Yet just as I was making my move, I heard a voice shout 'Brenda!'

Looking up, I see a youth about my age, barefoot and wearing a long black mantle, clinging to a cross on a plinth. He is using a toothbrush to clean between the marmoreal fingers of a half-life-sized Roman centurion, cruelly engaged in giving Jesus a Chinese burn to get him back to his feet.

'Simon!' said Brenda 'what are you doing up there?'

He laughed and it seemed to me that I could no longer exist as she ventured into duologue with him, ignoring me. He ignored me.

I never saw her more animated. Whereupon I dumped her and took up with a Sydney girl, though we did eventually marry. It was probably nothing more sinister than glamourous newsreader chats with bland weatherman under final credits, but you never forget the face of a rival, not at that age, if he's platinum-blond.

It was surely Simon Bourke, who on profession took the name 'Simon of Cyrene', which is pretty much the same name, but seeing his stat dec had been conferred on him by Mercy Sisters, it may have been some kind of twisted tribute he was making them, who would know. He was a creature of the Catholic Church, our Reverend Rocky Buzzacott.

And always I see him clinging to that Ninth Station, Jesus Falls a Third Time.

> Can be hard in the retard yard to scab a tab of eccy
> While finding little boys to woo would take a deal of reccy
> But 'pon my soul if that's your goal you've not been thinking clearly
> You don't need pill or partner should you judge yourself sincerely
> Let execution then proceed
> A smidge past the last-minute reprieve

Fall of the House of Paul

Mumbles died powerless, and don't we mostly? Can you suppose Don Bradman, up the road there in Bowral, the greatest sportsman who ever lived, with batting average four standard deviations from the international mean, succeeded in putting from mind he'd scored a duck in his last innings? No one draws comfort from what he used to be.

The day after Mumbles' funeral I returned to Kenmore Cemetery, formerly St Patrick's Cemetery, to inspect the headstones on Craig's Hill. The Gothic chapel, extended to incorporate smokestacks and catafalque, was once the Marulan Catholic Church. The date '1869' may still be seen on the stone tympanum. In 1937 the church was moved to its present location to become the mortuary chapel for the local religious. One of the still-extant stained-glass windows was donated by the Sisters of Mercy, another by the Sisters of St Joseph, a third by the Christian Brothers, a fourth by the Sacred Heart Sodality, a fifth by the Children of Mary. They remain, as it were plucked from the bowl of eyes on a taxidermist's bench, as the property of Sidney Craig Funerals. In 2005 the Church sold the chapel for use as a crematorium. The bones of Cork-born Bishop Barry beneath the floor were disinterred and the statue of St Patrick, widely considered a remarkable likeness, removed. Most of St Patrick's Cemetery had already been sold to the Council but a moiety was retained by the Church, so that spilling down the slope of Craig's Hill today you will see the remnant of an era now dead and buried as the folk beneath, for no more Sisters of Mercy depart Westport, County Mayo, and no more local graziers' daughters put their hands up for a life of unpaid labour. Australian nun population peaked in '66 even as traditional garb was being replaced, post-Vatican Two, initially by that laughably cut-down version, soon to be binned entirely.

I was looking for the grave of a certain Mercy Sister which, when I found it, implored me 'Pray for Sr Mary Bridget Poidevin', which I did. I learned she 'died 15/7/86. R.I.P.' which was the day after the day I began work at Goulburn Gaol. The headstones of religious don't give you the date of birth or profession (item: not true of the Galong Redemptorists). There are more than two-hundred Mercy Sisters, Sisters of St Joseph and Sisters of St John of

God buried in Kenmore Cemetery and from the late 1940's the family name is included on the headstone: 'Pray for Sr Mary Josepha Coen, Sr Mary Juliana Johnson, Sr Mary Aquinas Chalker'. Prior to this Mercy nuns were stripped, in death as in life, of original sin: 'Pray for Sr M Baptist, Sr M Magdalen, Sr M Columba'. The most recent religious grave I saw was that of Sister Mary Lucina Burt, who died in 2007, the least recent that of Sister Mary Teresa, who died in 1871. There are eight-hundred-odd Mercy Sisters more or less alive in Australia today, none I imagine Celtic youngsters and many of them very old women. Madeleine Lawrence RSM, *Religiosa Soror Misericordiae*, died in 2012 at the age of one-hundred-and-ten, having entered St Michael's Novitiate and Scholasticate in Kenmore Street Goulburn in 1919, an era when the Code of Canon Law specifically forbad a Church funeral being given anyone about to be cremated. Maddy died at Mt St Joseph's, the Mercy retirement convent in Young, up the hill on Campbell Street from the now-abandoned, sadly-derelict Mercy Care Hospital, which served briefly as a backpackers' hostel for itinerant cherry-pickers. They thought for a time they'd sold it and broke out the Guinness but the cheque bounced. Mercy Sisters, six of whom sailed from Ireland in 1859 to take up initial residence in the stables of the Goulburn presbytery, ran St Michael's Novitiate House until the year 2000. Built around a granite homestead dating from 1873, the complex today comprises three two-storey buildings holding a great many Spartan bedrooms ('cells') and some dormitories, all alas with shared facilities, a number of small caretaker-style cottages and stable-style outbuildings, generally weatherboard, a courtyard and a tennis court. The old milking shed with extensive acreage running down to a picturesque bend in the Wollondilly River, think Abbotsford Convent in Collingwood on a similar bend in the similar Yarra; memories of Clonmacnoise on the Shannon? Hardly: nuns had to live outside the wall there, was sold by the Church in 2000. No shortage of takers and today consists in a housing estate with a dedicated riparian park and a view of the Police Academy, where freshly-minted rozzers throw their caps in the air. The five remaining Goulburn Mercies live in a clutch of villa home units two blocks down Grafton Street from the Black Joeys' Convent. They wear mufti. Not so much as a rosary, not so much as a badge to be seen, just the usual short, unveiled blueish hair and twin set. From 2000 to 2011 St Michael's Convent, subject to heritage order, limped along in the usual style as the furthest thing from a luxury resort, conference centre cum retreat house in a city where the best restaurant in town remains the Thai in the Bowlo, till after ten years on the market, having been passed in at auction on numerous occasions, it sold in 2014 to the Antiochian Orthodox Church.

To my north across a lawn beam cemetery I see a water tank amid eucalypts and against the wire fencing, fluttering in the wind, scattering in the sleet, plastic floral tributes of mauve, yellow and blue that have blown away from their companion toy windmills. To my east I see on a hill our famous memorial lighthouse, of which we may boast there has never been a ship wrecked within purview of its rotating beam, while in the foreground is the Police Academy, indifferent in style as the rozzers it produces. To my west are the rolling hills of Middle Arm and the road to Roslyn, but to my south, beyond the electricity substation, over a myriad frames and trusses amid the bare, recently bulldozed earth of Merino Country Estate, with its blue portaloos and opalescent utes of the chippies and Colorbond roofing promptly affixed as soon as the frame and trusses are up, a few untidy conifers spring from a hillock like a gyre of hair on a wart and look down on the remnant of what in my youth was a fifty-acre garden, featuring vineyard and orchard, with a view I imagine pretty well unobstructed a century ago across the river to St Michael's Convent. It was in that terraced garden between 1955 and 1974, in which year they were transferred to the grounds of St Michael's Convent, stood the fourteen white Carrara marble Stations of the Cross, clinging to the Ninth of which I first saw Reverend Rocky Buzzacott. And behind the tatty conifers, Ravenswood, a hilltop mansion purchased in 1896 for the Black Monks, the Congregation of Discalced Clerks of the Most Holy Cross and Passion of our Lord Jesus Christ, a building which for eighty-four years and two-hundred-and-eighty-one professions served as the Australasian Presentation Retreat. The purpose of the Marys Mount Presentation Retreat / Novitiate House was 'to train priests by constant exercises of the spiritual life that they may be able to impart the light of truth, faith and hope to lost souls.' A worthy intent if mocked and vitiated in these dark days, as adduced by Father Superior John of the Adelaide Passionists, who presents himself on the Monastery website (not as, say Brother Stan hails from Port Lincoln, has been stationed in Marrickville, St Ives, St Kilda, many years PNG) but rather 'Good old Collingwood forever /

We know how to play the game / Side by side we stick together / To uphold the Magpie name / Hear the barrackers a-shouting / As all barrackers should / Oh the premiership's a cakewalk / For good old Collingwood'; and while it is true that in the nineteen-fifties religious vocation abounded on the NSW Southern Tableland, to the point it attained a level not seen since pre-Reformation Europe, and it wasn't only Celts, bearing in mind that at the time of the Tudor Spoiling of the Monasteries by Thomas Cromwell, de facto founder of the Anglican Church, fully one Englishman in five was a celibate in holy orders, it shortly thereafter disappeared as quickly as a felon espying an empty wheelie bin by the main gate. For from 1969, or about the time the newly-developed contraceptive pill began widely to be prescribed by the medical profession to unmarried girls, until the building was sold by the Church in 1974, what had optimistically expanded to become a heritage-listed, forty-bedroom monastery housed four tenants, the platinum-blond Father Simon of Cyrene Reverend Rocky Buzzacott, his father superior, a novice master and a single novice who subsequently dropped out as most, unhappily, did.

I mean, would you be wearing sandals today? Try two a.m. on bare boards and lino.

I am happy to report that Ravenswood is now back on the market under instruction of the receivers as twenty-five very affordable strata home units, some with views, not to be sold in one line but fully compliant, Alhamdulillah, with existing fire regulations. The land on the slopes below was sold decades back to developers so that the monastery belltower, empty of bells, is now surrounded, as prophesied, with housing estates. Presciently, the last Father Superior, Gerard Mahoney CP, *Congregatio Passionis*, had the remains of twenty-two Passionist fathers and brothers exhumed from the monastery graveyard, under supervision of local police and health department officers, and reinterred in Rookwood. 'They would not wish their graves to remain in the middle of a housing settlement,' he said at the time.

Oh come on Gerry it could be worse! They could be in the shadow of a crematorium. And what could be more cheerful to the long-celibate soul than the peal of a child's voice? Within earshot of the graveyard, now bulldozed beneath the AV Jennings Ravensworth Heights Estate, we have not one but two childcare centres disturbing, with their lurid billboards, an otherwise unbroken expanse of pristine private dwellings; Kids Choice Childcare Centre at the bottom of Ben Street and Starshine Childcare Centre on the Marys Mount Road end of Barry Crescent off Monastery Drive.

Want more pay to spend all day confined to an enclosure
Wiping bots of tiny tots made ill through their exposure
To mortgages worth half a mill a single wage could ne'er fulfil
Whose mothers say 'Enjoy your day we can't afford to knows ya'?
Wipe a riper bot my friend
I have a butt I'd recommend

Leave it at that

And it's not just Marys Mount, but every hill around Goulburn is graced with a dilapidated mansion. They squat like flies preening their forelegs on cowpats. West of the northbound golden arches on the road to Grabby, past what was St Patrick's College, we have Bishopthorpe, a tribute in bluestone gabled bays to the medieval English bishop's palace, in recent years a luxury hotel that cost a motza to refit and left local tradies thousands out of pocket when it couldn't pay its way; I mean, would you want a five-star holiday in Goulburn even with complimentary ghost tour? Now distinguished by a wholly superfluous 'Keep Out' sign at the entrance to the drive. Built as a residence for Mesac Thomas, first Anglican bishop of Goulburn, it housed briefly an Anglican order of monks. Between 1921 and 1941 the Anglican Community of the Ascension and the Roman Catholic Congregation of Discalced Clerks of the Most Holy Cross and Passion of our Lord Jesus Christ, the last in their black woollen habits the first Roman cenobites to be sighted, post-Reformation, on the streets of London, this around 1840, could eye each other's monasteries over the Chinamans Flat. Ascensionists, however, could scarce compete with the tubular bells of the Passionists, a full octave originally housed in the Sydney GPO but disposed of as insufficiently plangent for the din of Martin Place, so that Bishopthorpe the monastery, effectively deserted at the outbreak of World War Two, was dissolved in 1943. I don't think it ever had many tenants but a father and a brother from the community were exhumed from the Bishopthorpe graveyard in 1996 and reinterred east of the tower in the south-eastern wall of St Saviour's Anglican Cathedral.

Gabled bays bring to my mind Munster's Mt Melleray Abbey, which fairly bristles in them, like a sink overfull of detergent, and the Mt Melleray Order of Cistercians of the Strict Observance, OCR, *Ordo Cisterciensium Reformatorum*, was bequeathed eight-hundred acres of Goulburn land in 1888, a tidy parcel, later relinquished through perceived dearth of a local postulancy for the Trappist lifestyle.

And the donor was a cousin of mine.

Could they have civilized us, the White Monks? They'd have had a crack. Giraldus Cambrensis writing at the turn of the twelfth century, the golden age of the Cistercians, the age of the Abbot of Clairvaux, of whom it was said that mothers hid their sons and wives their husbands when he was about, though he cautioned he would have all men accepting his Benedictine rule leave their bodies at his gate, says of their impact on the rude Welsh: 'Give them a wilderness or forest and in a few years you will find a dignified abbey in the midst of smiling plenty.' Plus a few men who despite a pabulum of beech leaves and beer are literate in Latin. Perhaps the problem was not so much the delectable beers they brew (viz Chimay, 'look dear I'm only having one', stocked at Jim Murphy's Airport Cellars, afizz with abbey well water and Father Theodore's yeast) as the Strict Observance: nothing to smile over there when breasting a bar. A pocket of silence hereabout would be quickly dealt with. No silence in Grabben Gullen. No silence at the Albion, which is pretty much all that remains of old Grabby. Breast the bar as a thoughtful silent man at the Albion, you'll hear the words in no time, 'Ya got a name?' Whilst outside the pub the grapevine has withered. I didn't know my grandfather had died till a week after the funeral. Inside the pub, as you'd expect, it's yap yap yap, they never let up. Christ, how I hate the sound of the human voice! Talk is the human spirit, according to Samuel Beckett, but we need to overcome it or risk ending up, as Samuel Beckett did, a gibbering head in a bin. Silence is the means. I am wholly in favour of penitential silence as practiced at Port Arthur's Benthamite Prison, which warders patrolled in felt slippers communicating through sign language. Port Arthur's Separate penitents were kept strict one-out in total silence. Even at compulsory attendance in chapel they were kept isolated in separate stalls, one-out in their own personal exercise yards. Goulburn was built in the style of The Joy in Dublin to accommodate the Crofton system in which the felon did solitary for the first nine months of his sentence and untoward speech earned him a hardwood gag; but those days, sadly, are over. To cite St Isaac of Nineveh: *Above all love abstinence in speech for it brings you nearer the fruit. The tongue cannot express it. First of all let us force ourselves to abstain from speech; then from this abstinence will be born in us something which leads to silence itself. When you put on one side of the scales all the works of this life of a monk and on the other silence you will find the latter outweighs the former.*

Bentham's original categories of 1791 still appertain: daring raw offenders, quiet raw offenders, decent females, dissolute females, daring old offenders, quiet old offenders and thoroughbred offenders.

We are not, thankfully, wholly devoid of holy men in Mulwaree, for we have our Orthodox Antiochians, and the Holy Cross Seminary of the schismatic Society of Saint Pious the Tenth (SSPX), just a few klicks down the Braidwood Road from Wakefield Park where you get your backside trackside, is very much in business in this Year of Our Lord 2015 as it dates from post-Vatican Two. Housed since 1988 at Inveralochy, the usual dog's breakfast of incongruent structures sprawled around a hilltop homestead built in 1833 that became St Michael's Agricultural and Trades College, run by the Christian Brothers, who siphoned off most of the orphans from St John's Boys' Orphanage, run by the Mercy Sisters; thereafter a WHO drug rehab; if you took a mass there Sunday morning the priest would both turn his back to you and speak in Latin. The liturgy is deemed to be between the priest and the Lord and I am there to eavesdrop. A layman is but an intruder. The purport of the SSPX, according to its website, is 'the priesthood and all that pertains to the priesthood and nothing but what concerns it'.

But the most prominent hilltop building you will see as you whiz down the Hume, watching out for rozzers who hide beneath Windellama Road, is the nursing home used to be Gill Memorial Home for Boys, operated by the Sallies between 1936 and 1979, that two-storey building of dark brick with the tower at the summit of the Auburn Street hill, one block up from the huge ex-St John's Orphanage, heritage-listed now fire-damaged haunt of druggies and taggers. You can see the Gill building from the CBD as well as from the Hume bypass. It was in the Gill building during the nineteen-sixties and -seventies that foundlings as young as six years were routinely anally raped and 'tortured' (which just means flogged, put in cages, made to eat their own vomit, stand in the dining room with soiled sheets on their heads if they'd wet the bed, that kind of thing, forget the 'torture', bad boys need correction) by various Salvation Army male personnel, according to evidence recently presented to the Royal Commission into Institutional Responses to Child Sexual Abuse. At A-wing in protection where rockies while away their days, they mix with each other but not with other inmates, the modern warder's job being largely to protect inmates from other inmates. Rockies — rock spiders, pedos — have urine and faeces hurled at them, are jibed and spat at by other inmates and classified by other inmates as 'putrid' 'very putrid' and 'very very putrid'. A man who has raped a six-year old boy would be classified 'very putrid'.

And so platinum-blond Passionist Father Simon of Cyrene Bourke, an orphan

from St John's who headed for the Presentation Retreat rather than St Michael's
Ag and Trade upon graduation to year four from St Brigid's School, run by the
Mercy Sisters, thereafter St Patrick's College, run by the Christian Brothers, the
last a cesspit of paedophilia on a par with St Stanislaus in Bathurst, was a regular
buzzacott, as evidenced by his fellow felons having classified him as 'very very
putrid'.

That said, I never saw his case file. I couldn't find his warrant file and I don't
know, if he's buried, where. It isn't Rookwood.

Often in denial and frequently in tears; that's your typical rocky. Bourke
would have been about as popular with fellow scumbags as Pell's housemate
Gerald Ridsdale, the priest who in 1982 installed a fourteen-year-old boy in his
Mortlake presbytery bedroom.

A mullion from a gabled bay at Cappoquin in Munster
A rosary of ebony, an omega and alpha
Embroidered on a chasuble the colour of alfalfa
No longer cut the mustard for Breadalbane or Taralga
But say what you will of Sister Pat
She'd spank your arse and leave it at that

*While you still have eyes, before they are covered in dust, fill them with tears. To mourn
and shed tears is a gift of the passionless. If the tears of a man who for a time weeps and
mourns can not only lead him to passionlessness but even completely clear and free his
mind of all memory of passions, what can be said of those who day and night exercise
themselves in this doing with knowledge?*

St Isaac of Nineveh

Last minute reprieve

And there was none, despite the pleas of our parliamentarians when Indonesia executed two Australian traffickers, Andrew Chan and Myuran Sukumaran, old boys, like Roger Rogerson, of Homebush High. They were shot dead by firing squad at the hour of Vigil on the prison island of Nusakambangan, prompting a Twitter explosion and retaliatory withdrawal of our ambassador. Chan, a decade on death row at Kerobokan in Bali, had become a Christian pastor and mounted the cross singing Worship His Holy Name. He first shook hands with his warders. Sukumaran converted to Christ as well but in his last hours and I don't doubt the sincerity of either man's conversion as I believe it the outcome of a successful stay on death row. We must through much tribulation enter into the kingdom of God. Van Tuong Nguyen, another Australian trafficker hanged in '05 in Singapore, also became Christian in the shadow of the scaffold but dare I say it, remove that scaffold and you remove the incentive to repent. Why not execute Vincent Stanford who raped and murdered Stephanie Scott? He freely admits it, doesn't regret it. At twenty- six, his life sentence without parole for fifty years will cost the taxpayer upwards of two million dollars. We know in theory we are bound to die. Death row brings it home. Chan married, the day before he was shot, his local sweetheart and comforted those who died alongside him, leading them in two hours' preparatory prayer. Blindfolds were refused and a pastor who witnessed it said she'd never seen eight felons die so well. They do them in batches of eight.

Said the *Oz* editorial 'Indonesia has not only lost international prestige in this senseless act, it has squandered the potent example of two rehabilitated men. As the Foreign Minister has argued, here was a case where the Indonesian penal system had a resounding success. Chan and Sukumaran were the embodiment of redemption. Moreover they were using their talents to improve the lives of prisoners and to increase the possibility that they would not reoffend. Chan had become a pastor and spiritual adviser to other inmates; Sukumaran found peace in art and used it as a transformative act for him and others in incarceration. Alive even if serving life sentences, they would have been exemplars in countering a dehumanising system. In death they call to mind the callous approach of some Indonesian officials.'

But Indonesians always laugh where others see nothing to smile at, even as the bane of the backpacker, Ivan Milat, greets you with a grin. Bali bomber Amrozi was in stitches throughout his trial. Tony Trimmingham, CEO of Family Drug Support, says 'perhaps their greatest regret will be what they have put their families through.' In his magazine *FDS Insight*, Trimmingham, who lost a son to heroin but opposes capital punishment, writes 'We believe the families of these two men have suffered already the shock of finding out, the hope and despair they have gone through over the past ten years. The imagination of this cruel and barbaric death. The pain that will never go away. Waking from dreams of them being alive to the nightmare of the reality of their deaths. The birthdays and anniversaries. They are sustained by support now but that will vanish in time. Then the shame and stigma and thoughtless and ignorant comments of others.' It was the families of the felons I felt for, with their endless to-ing and fro-ing, their nights in the cheap Goulburn motels, the inevitable self-doubt, the squatting and coughing. The appalling spectacle of Sukumaran's mother being papped and jostled in Java cried out for brush and easel, yet all we got from Myuran was his Quiltyesque self-portraits.

I don't like Quilty's work. He had an exhibition at the Goulburn Gallery shortly after he won the Archibald, all cars and budgerigars. When it comes to Archibald winners I far prefer Keith Looby. I wonder what happened to Keith.

The crime in the case of Chan and Sukumaran was significant. In 2005 the Bali nine, who had shuffled through Denpasar airport with thighs like Maori back-rowers, mostly mules but superintended by Chan and Sukumaran, whom a little bird has told me were on their eighteenth visit to Bali, were busted through an AFP tip-off with eight-point-three kilos of uncut premium slow, worth a conservative four million in the seller's market of the mid-noughties, all destined to be cut and wrapped in the unit blocks of Cabra. I have been told by men who would know there is no thrill compares to smuggling slow through an Asian airport but even without that eight-point-three, one-hundred-and-thirty-one Aussies OD'd on slow that year, including a few of mine. You find them cold and blue in the slot, fit still in the vein, often as not in a foot. There's gear aplenty inside but mostly cut with gyprock. Good gear wreaks havoc.

I'd have given Chan and Sukumaran a hot shot with their uncut gear, death by lethal injection, as advocated by Buwas, head of Indonesia's Badan Narkotika

Nasional. Let the punishment fit the crime. And I don't believe a condemned man should be given ten years on his Road to Damascus. If you are condemned to death in China you are taken from the courtroom and shot, so that your family, while billed for the bullet, is spared years of agony but that's not what I want to talk about as I had an instructive day yesterday. I'd rather speak of that.

> Andrew Chan and Sukumaran declined to wear a blindfold
> Took the bullet to the chest in confidence that they would rest
> Their head against the Saviour's breast before the sun had risen
> And grant us your peace O Lamb of God
> We seekers of peace who will drop on the nod

East Coast high

An East Coast Low, effectively a cool slow-moving cyclone, sat over the coast all last week and devastated with flash floods the Hunter, which is the only break in the whole, mostly heavily-wooded Great Divide, though round Crooky and Grabby where I live the Great Divide is farmland. It was a monster. Several Dungog residents drowned as vehicles were swept off causeways and a few Dungog aged-care units were washed away in a freshet.

An East Coast Low is a beast that never ventures far inland and we got hardly any rain in Grabby, while they received over nine inches in Wingecarribee Shire, known as 'the Southern Highlands' though actually nothing of the sort, only a tongue of the Central Tableland that abuts the coast as closely as the Tableland ever does. It's the shire to our north. You get a great view of the Pacific Ocean on the road from Robbo to Jamberoo, and yesterday you got a better view than had been offered in a century, but that said there was debris over the roads.

After a decent fall of rain accompanied by gale-force wind, the mood of the folk who live in what was once known as the Irish New Country, that Land of the Golden Fleece that stretches down the Central into the Southern Tableland of New South Wales from Bathurst to Goulburn, and out into the Central Western Slopes from Mudgee to Boorowa, lifts. Our local Rock Choppers got off to a poor start. The early Church in this colony was exclusively Anglican. The first three Irish priests, Fathers Harold, O'Neill and Dixon, arrived as convicts after involvement in the insurrection of 1798. Father Dixon, wearing vestments of curtain fabric and holding a tin chalice, celebrated the first Australian RC Mass in 1803. After the second Vinegar Hill rebellion the following year, permission to celebrate Mass was withdrawn and the three priests repatriated. Next on the scene in 1818, Cistercian Father O'Flynn, was appointed directly from Rome but gaoled on arrival as a common felon.

Such disrespect would needs disappear in the wake of the Liberator, a stained-glass portrait of whom may be seen under the Irish holy trinity of Brigid, Columba and Patrick (Columba given a Roman tonsure) in the Irish- imported south window at St Patrick's Church Boorowa. Hurrah hurrah for Boorowa, hurrah for Daniel O'Connell. 'Have you been to Ireland at all?' a young Mercy

Sister was asked. 'I have not,' she replied, 'but I have been to Boorowa.' By 1843 Sydney had a Roman Catholic archbishop who proved to be an Englishman from Downside Abbey. The first of our three local Irish-born bishops, William Lanigan of Tipperary, RC Bishop of Goulburn from 1867, would not be dictated to by an English recusant. The teeming schools and orphanages of Australia's oldest inland city would not be run by Dagos or Dom Poms on Lanigan's watch, but rather by Sisters of Mercy, founded Dublin 1831, and Christian Brothers, founded Waterford 1820; Daniel Mannix, nascitur Cork 1864, would prove the prudence of this decision, with an education fit for Mannix fashioning Simon Bourke.

My own surname Leahy is Irish, quite common in Munster, but I couldn't be less interested in my own ancestry. Come find me? No way. I felt at home in Ireland but that is a common sensation, carefully nurtured by the Bord Failte. If half the world didn't feel so at home in Ireland there wouldn't be an Irish economy, which said, I do have a sense of exile here at home on windy Willochra. I often think I'm back in Ireland, sometimes wish I were. I did feel at home in Kerry, Clare, Galway, Mayo and Sligo. More so than on Willochra, so what can it be I miss? It can't be the black pudding. It can't be the Ulster fry-ups.

It can't be Loreena McKennitt singing The Bonny Swans. It can't be Paul Brady singing Arthur McBride. It can't be Davy Spillane playing Caoineadh Cu Chulainn.

I see now t'is the light. I have had cataract surgery, yes, but all that haze before my eyes was not defective lenses. There are particles aplenty in the atmosphere but you don't appreciate the full extent of what vegetation contributes until you have had nine inches of rain in a week with storm-force gale. How your mood lifts when the sun emerges and the wind dies away, for the light is no longer your typical Australian light, a bit dusty, but rather the light of Connaught where you get an East Coast Low most every day; sharp, clear, well-defined. The leaves sparkle and there is depth to the umbra.

So it's not the craic and not the music and not the Guinness lager, it is the light. It is the North Atlantic light we so miss in the Irish New Country. This insight hit me yesterday just south of the town of Bundanoon as I was driving to Robbo. I suddenly felt less homesick. There stands in the Morton National Park just south of Bundy on the Penrose Road an exemplary stand of scribbly gum, hard-leafed scribbly, *E. sclerophylla*. All the snow-white trunks had decorticated in the wild weather leaving them smooth and naked and as I drove through these graceful creatures I saw their slender crooked limbs all oiled and glistening and thought to myself for the first time, how attractive. It was a moment. Whenever I visit Moss Vale saleyard to look at some store cattle, I've long turned off the Hume at Marulan and made my way through Tallong so I've driven through that singular stand of trees many times, and always reproaching myself I couldn't seem to see the beauty of which others spoke, and yet it was the light to blame. Truth to tell, it was the *trees* to blame, as they are pyrophytes, pumping out those droplets of flammable oil the better to ignite, and so it is largely eucalypt oil that renders the light of our Irish New Country so un-Irish.

In the time of Brigid, Columba and Patrick, Ireland contained not one single town. The population centres were the monasteries and the whole country was afforested with oak, ash, birch, rowan, yew, hazel, thorn. It is said you could walk on the tops of the trees, mostly sessile oak, from Letterfrack to Galway over what is today the bleakest bog in Connemara. Ireland went from being the most to the least afforested European state, while the Irishman, at one time the thinnest, has become the fattest European. I recall being moved to tears by the beauty of the forest round Muckross and yesterday I was moved to tears by the beauty of the forest round Bundaloony. It was a moment. No matter how briefly, something was laid to rest. I had to pull off the road.

It has to do with light. It *all* has to do with light, just as grace has to do with mood. God is Light with a face while mood is a matter of chemistry. Light is conditioned by wind and rain and we need to make friends with that light if we're not to keep squandering our hard-earned super on aviation fuel but we need perhaps a thousand years before this can happen. At present we expect North Atlantic light and seldom receive it.

Till yesterday, if you'd asked, I'd have said the only positive in growing old is the decreased intensity of grief at finding the first scratch on your new car, that kind of thing, but yesterday's insight impels me to make an adjustment to all I observe and amazingly — miraculously — the correction applies retrospectively. I have become more content at age thirty-one than I was. Mind you I did become *less* content at age thirty-one than I was, when at age forty-five I learned my wife had been screwing another man.

Flammable inflammable t'is all the same to me
Who never in all Oireland saw more beautiful a tree
Than the alabaster eucalyptus gum of Bundanoon
Escort yon gloomy piper and his fiddler from the room
And pour the whiskey down the sink but keep a bottle spare
In case the climate changes
And we've nothing left to wear

Hasta la vista

I departed Corrections in '06. Towards the end of what amounted to a life lagging without parole I was chair of the Goulburn pre-release committee that meets from time to time with DOCS to discuss pre-release programs. I recall the case of an old lag, early seventies, my present age, about to be released from the main. He'd spent half his life in custody and the question arose as to where he'd be housed, as he'd nowhere to go and we didn't want him knocking at the gate pleading for readmission, as happens. His young parole officer was reluctant to place him in a boarding house because he was old-school.

"'What would you do? I asked him,' she said 'if a paedophile lived on the premises? I'd kill him, he told me. I'm old-school.'"

That said, there would be positives. You could be pretty certain that, like Mandela, he'd make his bed.

A man my age is risk-averse and barely capable of violence but he could gee someone up. As to the kiddie-fiddlers themselves, they are a proper headache. Should the *Daily Tele* sniff out their release and alert us to their whereabouts we may, in our righteous indignation, hound them from dwelling to dwelling, as happened in the case of both John Lewthwaite and Dennis Ferguson. Correctional Service Canada has Circles of Support and Accountability in which trained volunteers, ideally retired pastors, meet weekly with the core member, who is on parole and has a contract with his Circle not to reoffend, and chaperon him one-on-one; the eighteen sites in Canada, working with one-hundred-fifty kiddie-fiddlers, cost two-point-two million Canadian dollars in 2014. Cheaper to shoot them. But can they be cured of this one perversion we are not as yet minded to celebrate? There is no disputing their high rate of recidivism.

Since the introduction of Megan's Law by President Bill Clinton, a man with strong if confused views on sex, all registered US sex offenders, known as '290's' in California, must notify authority of any change in address and will be tracked on parole by GPS through mandatory anklet. As the more restrictive Jessica's Law became imminent, I felt no need soever to confer with US Corrections personnel but found myself doing so on account of — wait for it: honeybees.

No cultural leech-bite ever left me itching to visit the US West Coast. I do enjoy the music, Art Pepper through Frank Zappa, but American cinema is generally unsuited to viewers over the age of fifteen; *Batman, Superman, Iron-Man, Spider-man, Ant-Man, Wolverine, Hulk, Thor, Storm*; why no interest in the real superheroes like San Jose or San Diego? In '06 I was flat out in the ossuary, aka Kennelworth, still raising poll Herefords, not quite ready to acknowledge the judging ring has ruined the breed, but growing weary, starting to feel pins-and-needles in the limbs, when brother Pete, who has five-hundred hives close by the pines of Black Springs (to put that in perspective Richard Adee of South Dakota has twenty-three-thousand hives, and so Pete has become yet another late-onset baggy, in his case Oberon, a one-hundred-bed, minimum-security Young Offender prison), told me he'd been speaking to a mate from Blayney who'd been sending bees abroad, and who'd expressed the view that the recent Free Trade agreement with the US was an invitation to all beekeepers within a few hours of Kingsford Smith to stop thinking honey and start thinking bees. Sixty-million almond trees require a million hives and the fulminant Colony Collapse Disorder, CCD but known to Pete as PPB, Piss-Poor Beekeeping, whereby bees disappear as it were overnight, was rife in the US, which meant almond pollinators were keen to access stock and Australia, the only continent still free of varroa mite, was the only source. I'd worked with Pete in our halcyon days, driving the truck and transporting hives using ramp and trolley; no fork lift or pallets for Pete, and well I recall how one dark night we drove over a set of harrows and had to unload and reload two-hundred cranky three-deckers, all spewing angry workers and dribbling yellow-box honey as Pete did his extractions at home using a manual centrifuge — and we still caught up weekly on the blower, and when he confided how dearly he wished he could visit California, I said, well I can concoct a reason to visit California, let's go. So we journeyed together to the Golden State. I took two weeks' study leave, he'd been to Bali, he had a passport, he took a protracted sickie, he drove down through Burraga and Binda to Grabby and off we went on a train to International Airport via Macarthur.

I was dreading the urinations on the long-haul flight as I'd just had radical prostatectomy at Calvary John James. It was hard to piss and hurt to piss and flow was intermittent. If only we could have been more accepting of people shoving their fingers up our asses.

Stage three; I'd been assured the dancer hadn't shimmied beyond the prostate: why then pins-and-needles in the limbs, toothache in the pelvis?

We flew as the bee flies, though unlike the bee with a return ticket, and packed into a seat rather than a box of compressed board and flywire containing a tin of sugar syrup and supplied with a mated, thorax-marked queen in a plastic cage, with two kilograms weight of our companions, one box per hive body, on pallet covered in dry ice, from Sydney to San Fran, home to all with which we must now contend, Silicon Valley. There we were not shaken forth like grass from a lawnmower grass catcher. Pete had brokers to see in Fresno and I was on a mission near there so we drove south about five hours till in our jetlagged stupor we imagined we must have overshot or taken a wrong turn as we drove into an airless valley entirely covered in thick yellow smog.

'Christ,' says Pete, 'this must be LA. Jesus, what a hole!'

But no, it was our destination, the San Joaquin Valley which, while technically a desert, is the food bowl of the US.

Leaving Pete in Fresno I turned west off Ninety-Nine and passed through acres of almond groves containing not a blade of grass. I sighted a mega-dairy, first I'd seen, though I understand the Chinese propose installing one near Orbost to ship the milk home in a bulk freighter. Ten-thousand units of production each giving round ten-thousand litres a year, to be knocked at the age of four or five after two to three lactations; again there was no grass to be seen, just thousands of Friesian (Holstein) cows, bags as bloated as dead piglets, muzzles dusted in GM soymeal, barely able to move, which is a waste of energy, chewing the cud and standing about on a concrete-covered field of filth next to an Olympic-sized slurry lagoon of their ordure. In this Land of Milk and Honey I could see no hives but Pete assured me the bees would be trucked in, holding their noses against the fungicides and fungistatics sure to be sprayed about them by Mexican immigrant workers when the almonds flowered round Valentine's Day, for their one-hundred-fifty-dollar-per-colony month-long pollination.

The Twelve Day Wonder my old man called the messmate stringybark flow. We get one if we get one round Valentine's Day in Grabby. Beautiful honey, dark golden, only partially candies. Had a flow in Ninety-eight another in Twenty-ten.

Two hours north of San Fernando Valley, capital of the world adult film indus-
try, an hour south-west of Fresno, birthplace of stove-top crystal meth, first
synthesized in Fresno by a gifted Hells Angel from nasal decongestant, nail pol-
ish remover, paint thinner and battery acid, is Coalinga State Hospital, which
opened in 2005 during the Gubernator's first term, at a cost of almost four
hundred million greenbacks. Yes, it leaves Goulburn in the shade. It has a mall,
a cafeteria, a softball field, a graphic design lab, a barber's shop, a bakery. If you
had the choice you would certainly do your time in Coalinga, which is not officially a 'prison' but rather a 'mental health facility'; same shit, different bucket.
The one-point-two million gross square feet of highly polished floor space sit,
surrounded by the one item I did recognize (razor wire), on three hundred and
twenty acres of irrigated desert. In a field nearby it looked as though a lettuce
crop was being harvested. There are fifteen-hundred beds in Coalinga, though
at the time of my visit — did I mention I hold a Master's in criminology from
Sydney Law School? They gave me a few credits and it sure put me in Ron's good
books (irony alert) — this holding pen for rapists and paedophiles deemed li-
able to reoffend on completion of a custodial sentence was less than half full. But
can it be lawful, I hear you ask, to detain a felon on completion of his sentence?
The US Supreme Court says 'yes' but only in the case of SVPs, 'Sexually Violent
Predators', a designation imputed by county court at the time of conviction.
Fewer than one-percent of the state's sex offenders are SVP but what intrigued
me, and the pretext for my visit, en route to Parole in LA (where crack-addict
whores walk the streets asshole-naked, answering the query as to what whores
would wear after their couture had been appropriated), the pretext being that
over two-thirds of Coalinga inmates refuse treatment, and I think we can call
them inmates, given they have musters and wear uniform. As successful completion of a five-phase program is the only way out, I wanted to see this program in
situ to learn what made it so dire; alternatively, what was it about the place no
one wanted to leave?

I had the answer to my last question: here surely was paedophile purgatory
if not paedophile paradise, that being a place where civilized folk would shake
their heads in disbelief that any civilized nation could have so stigmatized natural
behaviour.

An autumn sun was shining red through an orange-grey haze when, to the reek of fertilizer, pesticide, herbicide and silage-and-steer-shit effluvium, an Afro-American Mr Five-by-Five met me at the gate. He escorted me to an office where I got a bad feeling as the man to whom my letter of introduction had referred me, glanced at the letter, put aside the missive in contempt and swung his feet off the desk.

'Dud,' he says, 'how was your flight over?'

'Yeah not too bad, eh.'

'Oh goodness. I'm sorry to hear that. Did you get out to the Rock?'

'The rock?'

'Alcatraz. There's a ferry. Are you fine with bagels? I'm on order us some bagels Dudley. How you like your coffee?'

As we neared the end of our tour Dr Housman, a spitefully dynamic Confederate who avoided all eye-contact, said 'I'll arrange for Mr Scanlon to speak with us in the morning. Hey you look jet-lagged Dud. You're not taking this in. Why not go back to Harris Inn grab some zees? You're beat.'

'I am. I will. Is Mr Scanlon on the program?'

'He is five years into the six-year program. He started his program at Atascadero which is where SVPs were held before Coalinga.'

'Can I also speak with someone who is refusing treatment?'

'Ah. I'm not so sure those men would want to speak to you, Dudley.'

'They can't be encouraged?'

Dr Housman did not smile as we in Goulburn might.

'Shoot no they cain't be forced to do anything. Lazy sons of bitches want to sit around play cards all-day lift weights they can do that at taxpayer expense for the remainder o' their days 'cause if they won't own what they have done they ain't never goin' out that gate but I do exaggerate: when they get old and bent or when they are very sick with cancer they will be discharged you bet but I don't believe they can be cured. Do you believe they can be cured? What did your thesis say? Haven't had time to read it. No, we are about containment. We believe there is a threshold beyond which bad thoughts become bad deeds.'

'I'd agree with that.'

'Well you'd be a fool not to. Now I see where you run a ranch Dudley. Goddammit you're a cattleman! You'll be staying at Harris Inn. You should take a drive 'bout a mile up Harris Farm feedlot on Interstate Five it's the biggest meat operation on the whole West Coast Cowshwitz supplies meat to the In-N-out burger chain vertically integrated too pavement to plate. They hold over some hundred-thousand beeves and we can sure smell them at times'.

I did call by at Cowshwitz to see Friesian steers standing among the Angus, then back to the Harris Inn where I lay awake most that night, thinking through the feeding up of Friesian steers. Next morning, which proved to be Halloween, which we don't as yet celebrate in Grabben Gullen, I did speak to Mr Scanlon. He was a charming, personable man as kiddie-fiddlers go, mid-fifties. Dr Housman, who seemed to think I was a psych, cautioned me as we rose to leave not to believe a word I'd heard.

'Mr Scanlon is a goddamned liar. Isn't that so Mr Scanlon? Mr Scanlon's polygraph did not comport with his DSFI.' Mr Scanlon looked bewildered. 'I don't see how that could be,' he said. 'Well I do,' said Dr Housman.

We then looked in at a room where men were sitting in a circle talking but Dr Housman ushered me out saying, 'we don't need to listen to that. Shoot we've heard that before. Let's go down the engine-room.' As we walked, gathering pace towards the engine-room, Dr Housman gave me a brief run-down on the five-phase program.

'I'll focus on paedophilia Dudley as I recall that's your interest. On admission we evaluate an inmate psychiatrically. You understand we are being asked to evaluate the degree of mental impairment in a man who at the time of his trial was denied the defence of mental illness. Then if he wishes to participate in the program he must do a self-evaluation. We use the Derogatis SFI questionnaire because it has two-hundred-fifty-eight items and that's a lot of lies to tell. We also insist he disclose to us any sexual offence he may have committed for which he was never charged and we then run a polygraph. I'm no great fan of the polygraph but we all possess a natural hesitation to confess to crimes we feel we got away with through fear the information may be held against us at some future time. It's called self-interest and in my experience is the only lie a lie-detector will detect in a paedophile because the paedophile as you would know is an expert and practiced liar. It is part and parcel of who he is. It is intrinsic to his grooming technique. It is his greatest pride. It is his modus operandi. He is a liar. Please don't be deceived by Mr Scanlon. We could never know what he was thinking just from listening to him mouth off. See what I like about the penis, Dudley, aside from that cute little ridge, it don't never lie. Willy never lies to me. We can do an Abel Assessment for Sexual Interest, visual reaction time, but only if we need to determine target orientation. Mostly we just hone in on Willy. Inmates have their one-on-one sessions, they can spill their guts out in these groups but are they able to control their deviancy? Only Willy will tell us. Now what you are about to see I don't normally show. You'll soon see why. As it happens I run a few beeves myself Dud. Guess we understand each other. Hey d'you get up to Cowshwitz?'

We enter a darkened booth that has a screen against one wall. There are booths to either side of us, and as the door closes there is the kind of silence you get when a tall celebrity enters a room.

'Penile plethysmography will give me your hots and colds. I don't know how you do it back home but we use the volumetric method because it is very sensitive to low levels of arousal. It will work on a flaccid penis. PPG can tell me you're aroused even if you don't know you are. Of course once we hit your sweet spot if you're a man given to rape, well you probably prefer a complicit witness and you will go off the scale. We could use a circumferential transducer on you, which is the electromagnetic strain gauge placed around the shaft, but do you know, with this Jessica's Law coming in next month, I believe many 290s will end up on the streets of LA because they won't be allowed to live within two-thousand feet of a school or a park or a beach or a burger joint or frequent any area where children gather and that could be most any place, so where the hell they going to live? That is not my problem. But I do have a problem because at present most 290s are not SVP but that could change under Jessica's Law and the buck ends here. I can't let them out that gate if they're not dead to their deviancy. Shoot I've only let but one man go and he came back. You see this Dudley? This inflatable cuff attaches to the base of the shaft and the glass cylinder measures subsequent air-displacement as you get your hard-on or not. You could try it on if you like. No? That's the easy part. I need to determine your stimulus but first let me ask you this; how many cows out there at Cowshwitz would be conceived through AI?'

'Oh quite a few I guess seeing this is dairy central. Holstein steers I should imagine certainly. We don't keep them in Australia beyond a few days.'

'Quite a few you guess. And do you AI your own cattle?'

'I can. I have a crush in my yards it's just that while I'm holding down a full-time job it is convenient to keep bulls.'

'Of course it is. And do you collect semen from those bulls?'

'Shoot no. I don't have the set-up. I keep a small battery of bulls but guys like me buy a straw of semen and keep it in a nitrogen tank.'

'And how would that semen be collected? You see what I'm driving at Dudley?'

'Not really.'

'A bull does not look at a stick book. A bull is presented with a cow on heat and deceived by a human being but the human donor jerks off. The mostly healthy young medical student who supplies semen to an IUI program sits in a booth rather like this and jerks off into a jar. He deploys imagination.'

'You have the advantage of me, Dr Housman.'

'I was conceived in iniquity. Psalm Fifty-one. There are those among us who would argue masturbation is onanism, a mortal sin. By the same token my father among others would take a dim view of what you're about to see but I make no apologies Dudley because I say to him, you may not like it but you live in a democracy and that democracy has voted to provide fertile young women whose partners may be sterile the opportunity to conceive though that may require a little assistance from Satan. In like manner, society charges me to ensure a violent sexual paedophile will not, given the chance, reoffend. To that end I need a little help from Satan as well so without further ado Dudley.'

Dr Housman disappeared and shortly thereafter the screen lit up. I found out later he'd only gone into the next booth.

'So what did you think of that Dud?'

'That is the most dreadful thing I have ever seen. Fuck me dead, I could not watch it. Jesus man that poor kid! How can you do this? I need some fresh air. I don't know if it was faked or not. Would it matter?'

'It was a bad one. No they don't fake'em. Won't be no fresh air today Dud wind's blowin in from Cowshwitz. Let's go get some bagels. Please don't dwell on what you just saw. You did ask about the program.'

We ate our bagels in silence. Eventually I asked the obvious question:

'Where did you get that footage?'

'I have no idea. Somewhere in the Philippines I'd guess. Never saw it before. We don't record them we don't need to. It's a twenty-four-seven live stream.'

'You're joking! That kid was being harmed!'

'Yes and it would have been a parent with a child. Of course he would say to us now you condone abortion *gotcha*! We don't condone child abuse but we have SVPs to screen. How else are we to do it? Abyss Creations that start-up Sex-Doll factory in San Diego won't make kee-yids. Their dolls are not something else either; they are anatomically correct. I specifically asked their CEO to make me some silicon kids and he refused. He'll do you a cut-price headless doll as not all men require heads but he won't do a child. Are you familiar with the Dark Net Dudley? That was a feed off the Dark Net. Our Onion Router System Tor was designed by Naval Intelligence to allow its officers to communicate anonymously which was fine. Four years back it was released for public use via a free downloadable web browser which was not so good. What you just saw was wrapped in several layers of encryption then bounced round the world off a random series of complicit computers. I can't say where it's from. No one can. And it's not a commercial operation because child porn is exchanged only for child porn. A user passes through a defined sequence of encrypted urls but only with an administrator's permission. Entry is denied unless material is offered in kind.'

'So you offer material in kind?'

'Relax. We just got lucky. We compromised an administrator who slipped up and revealed a digital location, now listen: if I was you I'd get straight down to LA 'cause tonight is Halloween, a night of concern to Parole and not because the dead are walking the streets. Children are walking the streets. All 290s must stay in their home, assuming they have one, they may display no enticing backlit pumpkin in the window and Parole officers go round fixing a sign to their doors saying 'No trick or treat.'

I read where Gardaí in Ireland retire child protection officers after three years. Longer than that, they feel you'd be safer working on Ebola in a pair of Speed-os.

'Nah, don't think I'm up to driving all that way right now, might end up on the wrong side of the road.'

'Ok then, trick or treat. My assistant is in today, Ms Ucicky. She works with our heterosexual rapists and she is a regular muffragette, a San Fernando girl.'

'Might try on the glass jar. What would you say to that?'

'I would say if the cap fits Dudley and believe me the cap will fit and do you know why? 'Cause a rapist is just a normal man who doesn't believe in Judgement. All Godless men rape women if they think they'll get away with it and generally speaking they do. Nine times out of ten. Good odds. What is the answer? Legalization has been proposed and there is merit to the suggestion. Context. We think of men who murder strangers in time of peace as bad people but those same folks will be shot for cowardice in time of war if they refuse. Context. It's a matter of conjecture, rape, when you endorse fornication. Even a violent rape is an increasingly semantic question. Ideally you would like two witnesses, Matthew 18, and preferably four. 'No' means 'maybe' as well as 'no'. Some women like it rough. Some women like to be strangled by strangers. Marilyn Monroe towards the end of her life was cautioned by police for having sex with strangers on the streets of LA. Rape is an easy accusation to make and spunk sticks but most women will not report rape when they did not give consent. What prevents rape in my view, Dudley, is lack of opportunity and fear of consequences from a woman's kinsmen.'

I was bagelled out by the time I sat in that booth and put on a cuff. I was now wearing hospital uniform and Dr Housman introduced me to Ms Ucicky as 'Dr Leahy' though I don't think she was taken in. Had a nice ring to it though.

I was flaccid throughout and I don't imagine Ms Ucicky, a buck-toothed Betty Blue-type wearing a pair of denim dungarees over the body of a Kim Kardashian, was much accustomed to that. But when briefly she entered the booth — I'd been told it was crucial she appear in person before the video screened — to check the cuff had been properly affixed, she did glance at me in a manner open to interpretation, the kind of look an old man pays for dearly in a whorehouse.

What follows I have researched on the Google cloud. If it's wrong don't blame me.

For twenty minutes I sat mesmerized as Ms Ucicky's naked body was trussed up using a length of sisal rope by a Japanese nawashi, which is what they call a master in the art of shibari in Japan. This was no live stream. Ms Ucicky, an aspiring actress, had pre-recorded a number of appropriately stimulatory videos in the San Fernando Valley. In ancient Japan a samurai felt the need to aestheticize everything he did and his art of Hojo-jutsu, developed in the restraint and torture of hostages, eventually merged with kinbaku, the Japanese art of erotic bondage. Knots in the rope are so positioned as to stimulate acupressure points and from time to time the camera would zoom in on the face of Ms Ucicky who, by the time she was hog-tied, was also 'rope-drunk', eyes glazed. Contrarily, as he worked, the pupils of the eyes of the geekish rope-artist dilated as though plied with atropine. It was most interesting and very artistic, ideal for Hobart's Dark Mofo, but Ms Ucicky, when she returned to the booth to examine the read-out on the graph, had just one question for me:

'Have you had prostate surgery?'

'What, no signal to noise? Maybe you've lost it, Darl. Maybe I'm same-sex inclined. Why not run me a visual reaction time on Fassbinder's *Querelle?* Truth to tell I'm into dogs.'

'Shinji ties up dogs. No seriously, would you like Shinji to tie you up a dog? What type of dog you prefer?'

'Mexican hairless.'

She burst out with such an unexpected, plosive, phlegm-loose, rattling raucous laugh I had to smile and we spilled out of that booth in such merriment that Dr Housman said, 'You two been smoking that whacky weed in there?' I changed out of my overalls and when I'd gotten back to Harris Inn, all but overcome by the miasma from nearby Cowshwitz, part of the same conglomerate, I sat on the bed and cried some.

I was still thinking of Ms Ucicky on the flight home, wondering what her parents were like, whether she had a brother, whether she had a child, whether her father approved her, what her mother would think of how she dressed. I wondered what kind of music she preferred, what kind of books she read, if any, whether she was a good cook, whether she could play the piano.

After I'm done crying I go downstairs to the restaurant where I find a seat facing the door — a prison officer is never comfortable unless in a seat facing the door — drank a pint of watermelon lemonade, ate a hickory salt and brown sugar rubbed thirty-ounce prime ribeye with whiskey butter, and aborted the rest of the tour. I never did return to Goulburn Gaol (not entirely true; I bio in from time to time and do the odd shift as a baggy). I did fax in my report, in partial consequence of which we have at present in the NSW Parole System thirty-seven serious offenders on extended supervision orders, but that was the end of my spell behind bars. I handed in my duress alarm.

Mind you, I still call out 'Gate up!' whenever the doorbell rings.

'You know what your name means?' I said to Pete on the flight back. All Hallows Day. Bit of a theologian, Pete, he once drew my attention to the fact that Apis had to have been the only prelapsarian worker, as otherwise Eve could never have offered Adam that apple. 'It means "Rocky". Simon called Peter aka Cephas, the fisherman known as Rocky. Upon this fisherman known as Rocky, who walked out on his wife and kids, I shall build my Church. It's the only note of levity in the whole New Testament.'

'It's not much of a joke' said Pete. He thought for a bit then said, 'A fisherman can walk out on his fish. Had Rocky been a beekeeper, things might have been different.'

> The Santas and the Sans have run their course
> And Conan the Librarian eviscerates the bourse
> To build a sanatorium of Flavian dimension
> For Violent Sexual Predators
> Starring Woody Allen
> Directed by Polanski with book and music written
> By the syphilitic Joyce and the syphilitic Britten

How can we say that a man has attained purity? When he sees all men as being good and when none appears to him unclean and defiled then he is indeed pure in heart

St Isaac of Nineveh

A rare care-bear

Did you ever pass a school playground in a country town at lunch-hour only to see the children subdued and downcast and solitary and tearful and walking round in total silence? No, and you never will, but that's what the rockies' yard was like, the day after the DIC.

I was kept busy and as I'd never before seen the rockies' yard or any other yard, I paid its mood on that dull day no mind. There had been cheering and jubilation from the other yards but that was to be expected, given the heinous nature of the crime for which the Reverend Rocky Buzzacott had been interned, but I didn't know then what that crime had been as no one told me anything.

Later in the week as I was bringing in some teabags for Laid-Back Lester, I found him undergoing an air raid from the new three-pipper.

'What do you actually *do* in here?' the three-pipper was asking. 'Why are you sitting there like that with your feet on the desk reading a form guide?'

'Because I am on my tea break,' observed Laid-Back Lester. Glancing at the tacky ikon of the Virgin on his desk, he then sent up some ack-ack, which today might run, 'As to what I do here you see before you a Death in Custody report which I shall duly collate copy and scan for the CSNSW Investigative Branch as a file for their TRIM container as soon as I have in my possession all relevant paperwork. There has been a suicide. At the time of the incident I attended the location to confirm an attempted resuscitation attempt by the FRO then commenced and concluded a Crime Scene Time Log. I prepared and submitted a briefing note to the Duty Officer within the required two hours, I directed the FRO to remain on duty until he had completed his incident report, but as no other inmate appeared involved I did not initiate counselling. I reported the incident on the OIMS Incident Reporting Module and promptly telephoned the Goulburn Ambulance Station, the Goulburn Police Station, the Duty Officer, the Regional Assistant Commissioner, the General Manager CSNSW Investigative Branch, the State Coroner, Workcover NSW and duly obtained a report from Justice Health that enabled me to submit my 48 Hour Accident/Injury Notification Form Offenders/Non Employees to Workcover NSW though the decedent had not to my knowledge worked in industries. I informed the Commander Security and Investigations, the Senior Assistant

Commissioner Inmate Custodial Services, the Commissioner, the Assistant Commissioner Offender Management, the Regional Commander, the Minister's Media Relations Officer, the Departmental Media Unit, the Departmental Regional Investigation Unit, the Corporate Counsel Legal Services Division, the Director Inmate Classification and Placement and the Corporate Research and Evaluation Unit. Given the decedent did not identify as indigenous I did not contact the Aboriginal Legal Service or the Director Aboriginal Strategy and Policy Unit. Given the decedent was a monk in a monastery and prior to that a ward of an orphanage I did not liaise with the Chaplaincy Coordinator to identify a delegate to attend the home of an emergency contact person. I completed in timely fashion my own OIC report and am in the process of collating the alcohol and other drug officer's report, the medical report, the psychologist's report, the welfare officer's report, the correctional education officer's report and the parole officer's report. I await the chaplain's report. More generally, I chair the reception committee in this wing, I arrange for the reclassification of all inmates under the umbrella of both SORC and PRLC, I liaise with Cooma and Berrima, I facilitate all inmate program pathways, I process referrals, I chair the CMT meetings for the classo reviews, I liaise with the classification coordinator re results and implement the relevant paper trails on inmate conduct, I process random, target and program urinalysis procedures, I process summary discharges and send them to the joint record section at Silverwater, I initiate. . .'

'Oh shut the fuck up. Just get your feet off that desk! What sort of example does that set the baggy?'

'Here are your teabags, sir' I said after the three-pipper had sloped off and the feet were back on the desk.

'Why don't you go fuck yourself?' enjoined a not-so-Laid-Back Lester. 'Better yet take this request to the Catholic chaplain please and ask why I've yet to receive her DIC report.'

'And where would I find her, sir?'

'I don't know. Use some initiative.'

Built before the Boneyard, the front yards by the old main gate contained a number of cages, six for the one-out segros, naughty boys who'd misbehaved by verballing and/or assaulting officers — let the rebellious not exalt themselves — with a larger cage down one end for dogs on strict protection. Tosh and I would escort these dogs to and from their cage each day as they weren't considered safe in the A-wing yard. Lock-in was at three p.m. after dinner muster at two-thirty and rolling let-go, for those not working in industries, not before nine a.m., which meant that much of the gaol was locked down eighteen hours a day.

Imagine that: eighteen hours a day cooped up with the gronk.

I had no idea where to look for the Catholic chaplain. I was maundering by the front yards wondering where best to begin when one of the segro desperates in the cages called my name out.

'Hey Dud!' he says, 'over here a minute, Bruz!'

I did as bidden. I hadn't yet acquired the knack of seeing inmates as scum. That would come only after my first week on the job.

'Hear you're looking for Sister Bridge.' A bovver boy covered in prison tatts, he was gripping the bars of his cage like a man trying to fart for a cash prize. 'Tell her not to come back.'

'Why's that?'

''Cause she has let herself down. She won't be safe.'

'How do you mean?'

'Can't speak ill of a nun. Just tryin to do yez a favour.'

'And you say she's outside?'

'Look for her in the admin block opposite to where the warrant files are kept in the building outside the main gate to your right with the big chimney. That's where the chaplains hang, hey Dud; couldn't make a phone call for me, Bruz?'

Rocking up to the admin block I found the Anglican chaplain — Trev Ironside — small, pot-bellied, bespectacled, bent, with gold sleeper in left earlobe — sitting under a banderole reading 'For I was an hungered and ye gave me meat: I was thirsty and ye gave me drink: I was a stranger and ye took me in: Naked and ye clothed me: I was sick and ye visited me: I was in prison and ye came unto me. Matthew XXV 35-36.'

'Excuse me sir,' I said. 'I'm told you're the Anglican chaplain. Would you be able to tell me where I can find the Catholic chaplain?'

'Is it about the DIC?'

'It is. She needs to fill in her report.'

'I haven't seen you before, have I? You new to the job?'

'Yes sir. Began work this week.'

'Oh please don't call me "sir". I would be the lowest form of life in this gaol outside yourself. "The dumping ground of the clerical world," says Taft in '78.'

'I wonder if you could tell me where I can find the Catholic chaplain?'

'Yes, you already said that. I haven't seen her. I don't think she's been in. I doubt she'll be back after what just happened. Mind you, she'll be hard to replace. Bit of a young fogey. You never saw her?'

'No sir. Only began work this week.'

'Where?'

'A-wing.'

'Oh Chr— Are you in a hurry? I mean… right now?'

'Not really. Well no I… not really… I… shouldn't. . . .'

'Sit down. I'm here for the blue as well as the green. Sit down, Bruz.'

'I'm sorry but every time I shut my eyes…'

'You see it again. That's how it goes. You're in shock. You want to talk? My name is Trev.'

'I don't really want to talk, Trev. I'll be right in a moment. I will sit down though, thank you. Where would I find this woman? I do need to find her. She has to fill in her report. She's holding things up.'

'If you must go chasing after her, the Mercy Convent is just a short walk from the Gordon Hotel, Kenmore Street, but they'll replace her. They'd want the money. Mind you, there'll be no replacing Sister Bridget Poidevin. Has no one told you about her?'

'No sir.'

'Bad business this. Mind you, I've had to write a few reports myself this year just quietly, so I know what's involved. They don't call this place 'the Killing Fields' for no reason. The chaplain's report 'may include' but 'is not limited to' you get the picture: history of interaction, any significant contact, any recent unusual behaviour, overall involvement. The report you're chasing up, though, will make for interesting reading.'

'Why's that?'

'Because he was her confessor. And they never defrocked him.'

He was in prison and ye visited him not
Indeed I heard you shout out 'Rot in Hell!'"
As he was being taken to the prison from the dock
How sweetly sounds the final muster bell
He was the least of the brethren of the Christ
Who so kindly gave His precious blood for me
But two Hells Angels would visit him one night
Two Angels from Hell to set him free

Never bring the drugs to the money

Religion is the opium of the people

Have you red marks?

An officially atheist Vietnam would vie with Australia as the world's least religious state. That said it has a long Theravada Buddhist tradition, and back in '86, when the Vietnamese community was well-represented in Goulburn Gaol and Mary Bridget Poidevin was Catholic chaplain, there was no Buddhist chaplain to cater to the cultural needs of the Vietnamese. By the time I pulled the pin, twenty years on, we had a Buddhist chaplain who came in one day a week, unpaid, to conduct his masturbation make that meditation class. The problem was he had hair on his head and didn't wear a saffron robe. He couldn't speak Pali. He didn't have the right-shaped eyes. He was a lay white Australian who couldn't project the required presence and in a prison, as in a convent, presence is important. History shows us hierarchy is best expressed through dress. Inmates from the MPU, X-wing and the main wear greens sewn in situ in the textile shop, but Guantanamo-ISIS orange dignifies the man from SuperMax as he shuffles, cuffed and shackled, to the clinic. When the priest comes in from the Goulburn Greek Orthodox Church of St Panteleimon in Macalister Drive, just down the road from TAFE, our former PLC in View Street, he strides the yards in his chimney-pot hat, long black cassock and ponytail and he looks the part. He commands respect. His untrimmed beard makes him the envy of every prison officer, who must trim or remove his own beard in order to accommodate a respirator. The old-time Salvo melded into the blue by posing as a screw. Rev Trev wore a dog-collar. The imam who caters to our Bruthas Behind Bars, whether terrorista or rightly-guided Koori, bio's into Prislam in his crocheted kufi and long white linen thobe, but are we so blind as to what we daily see as we drive about our city, we no longer register our former Passionist Monastery, our former Mercy Novitiate, our derelict St Joseph's Orphanage, our derelict St John's Orphanage, our derelict St Brigid's School, our derelict Marian College, our rechristened St Patrick's College, our former St Patrick's Cemetery, our former St John of God Hospital, our ex-Catholic Cathedral, scaffolding rusted on as the tower awaits restoration of the Murphy bell? Has it slipped our erstwhile Erse-speaking minds our ancestry was transhipped to the New Country in chains? We can be reminded as was proven by the impact of Mary Bridget Poidevin, a genius in her understanding of the power of dress. In setting back the clock a millennium she made Rev Trev look pretty ordinary. It must have been quite a spell she cast and I'm sorry I missed her.

One ex-officer told me you could no more resist her spell than you can resist tickling the throat of the Penrose Produce Store cat who lies supine on the counter next to the till.

When first she appeared at the gate in the summer of '85 / '86 I'm told she could have been holding an oxy torch and a pair of bolt-cutters under those capacious sleeves that fell down past her hands. You couldn't see her eyebrows, as these were hidden under the coif, but a pair of red lashes gave the game away, glowing as they did like copper wire. Though beautiful and fecund she declined with a smile the duress alarm and the matter was not pursued by Governor Mumbles. Despite summer heat, which can be fierce in Goulburn, she wore a black serge habit with bodice in neat pleats under a leather cincture. Her flowing skirt had been unhooked from pleated bustle mode so as to spread behind her in a train. Seen from behind, wearing the wide black veil folded to create pleats held with safety pins and stiffened with a piece of board, she might have been one of those Muslim women pushing prams round Punchabowl. Taking the weight of the veil over her white-coif-covered head and falling down so as to seal her ears, a white linen dimity parted upon her bosom to reveal the guimp, that starched white wimple of flat linen.

To the right of her cincture was a ring from which depended a rosary, well-worn, with an ivory and ebony cross, while at the centre of the cincture on the wrong side was a pouch, into which she had shoved a large wooden crucifix the size of a nunchuk. This crucifix attached to a cord that went around her neck beside the dimity.

'Hello!' she said to the gate in her Irish brogue with a smile to melt the heart: 'Can you guess who I am?'

He could. He was down on his knees and crossing himself. He was praying in mussitation. She had to bless old Costello before he'd open the gate and that was just the beginning.

She went on to win the hearts of the gaol, blue and green alike. There was no orange at the time: SuperMax opened in '01.

Catherine McAuley had wanted to help the destitute and needy
But she wasn't Roman Catholic as she came from a Quaker family
And the men who controlled the women said you cannot be a provider
Until you become RC and found a religious order
And your little Quaker mobcap must become an instrument of torture
All this conveyed me by Sister Edmund, beldam in a blue marcel
As we awaited the muster bell
By the time I professed said Edmund I was very good with a pin
I could remove the entire caboodle as a unit and put it back again
So I purchased a milliner's hatstand which I set on a tall bar stool
And my veil my coif my dimity and guimp
Would sit all night at my bedside like a disembodied ghoul
One full moon as I slept in my cell I heard a voice say 'Rise
And go across to the window
And tell me what you see there wit' your own two eyes
Have they aught to eat on Baggot Street?
Is the Liffey yet fit to drink?
Are the swells who stroll St Stephen's Green
Concerned what the poor might t'ink?
Is the sewer after being repaired?
Is the drunkard still lying in the lane?
Are the children being taught to read and write?
Has there been a break in the rain?
Ah no I said I see none of that
But the moon is on Marys Mount
And the monks have set a light upon the hill
And I hear their midnight chant
And the fourteen Stations of the Cross
Are shining under the moon

And the brilliant Wollondilly River
Is singing them a quiet tune
Oh said the voice where am I then?
You are far from home I replied
But the Christ was born in the Holy Land
And not by Liffeyside
You are in the New World where men's eyes
Are fixed upon the Old
So that every birth is a stillbirth
And there's no new tale may be told

How to forget the name of your first pet

By mid-'07 I had a revised diagnosis. I had the new prognosis as well, MPC M1b, metastatic cancer spread to the bone. No cure. Put your affairs in order. I said, well that could take time as I've a few jobs still need doing and some need doing again. I did resolve while driving home from Canberra's Deakin Oncology that day, I'll have no more Kee-mo. I'll never see a radiologist again as it's not compulsory. Further, I'll have no more of this funeral plan tele, which is all you seem to see on free-to-air. Your finger's never off the mute. That's three times I've been round the Scottish Isles in a year. I've had enough of the Dales and the Arctic and Amazonian rainforest. I'm wearying of the Serengeti, tiring of the Galapagos. I can't walk another English canal.

We had two feet of snow that night. By morning I'd resolved to buy a large satellite dish and remove the sign by the gate that read 'Willochra Poll Herefords, bulls for sale, all agents welcome'. It's easy to forego funeral plan tele when there's no power.

We had two feet of snow again last spring. It brought down the power lines but not the big white windmills that are my principal source of income since I dispersed the herd. They were still there, flexing the fibreglass. There'd been a sheep grazier's alert and I do have sheep on Willochra, not mine as the only creatures stupider than sheep are the people who keep them. I hadn't heard any snow as I downed my last dram of Laphroaig, but then again snow falls pretty quietly.

Prison staff of the district would have been overjoyed. You beauty, they'd have been thinking, we won't have to go to work today and they didn't, because the barrier 'road closed' was up on the Goulburn Road by the Crooky showground, under a flock of grass parrots clinging stiffly to the wires next to a festoon of lace-joined joggers. But that only stopped prison staff: everyone else drove round it.

Including me, in a pair of stylish ray bans as I had to fetch in hay. My store cattle wouldn't put their heads down in the snow and I couldn't get to the shed. I'd spent the best part of the morning shovelling out the ute. I'd been told to go easy there through fear of breaking a bone, but seven years had now passed since I last saw a doctor and I seemed to be still alive, though it can be hard to tell. The Cypress pines along my drive were showing me some respect but the wattles and the snow gums in the windbreaks fared less well. There were masses of limbs down. Merinos, fortuitously unshorn, were chewing at the wattle and I was surprised to see how daintily they can skip through the drifts, the more as my liquorice all-sorts cattle were standing in bitter complaint. I drove out to bludge a few bales of hay off Twomey. The Lord uplifteth all those who stumble but I did my knee as an SPO when a Maori broke my jaw. I was wired up for six weeks and did an MCL, while the bastard who did it got three months for assault to be served concurrent, which meant he cut his three months out while doing gaol time for his priors.

Twomey and I help each other out as necessary. Many a chore around the farm requires two pair of hands: bleeding the hydraulic brakes, wall-mounting a dryer. Twomey has a weakness for goats and recently scored himself five feral Boers that had strayed into a yard out Tuena and found themselves trapped. Twomey raced out with his float. On his return I was summoned to climb into the float with him to hold them by the horns as he drenched them and clipped their hooves. We worked with all the precision of a primary school brass band.

Driving cautiously, snow-blinded when some young prick sped by, I made my way to Twomey's shed which is just past the Pejar Road where Pejar Road dips down towards Kialla. Normally, I'd have driven up Pejar Road from Range Road, but I wanted to stick to the tarmac, though the snow at this stage was powder pure, wouldn't wet the hooves. Two days later, ice, but the fields remained a picture, the neglected hawthorn hedging particularly fetching. There were pockets of snow in the shelter belts a full week later. The temperature never rose above six degrees all week. It was a right dumping, the biggest since '88, extending all the way up the Great Divide to Stanthorpe in Queensland. And this just last winter.

After I'd loaded the hay I sat for a time to take in the view, listening as I did to the scherzo from Bruckner's ninth as repetitiously as ever did Erland Josephson in Bergman's *Saraband*. Many a two-part snowman was now going up by the road. The schools were closed so parents were bringing kids out for a frolic. How beautiful the lakes and dams with the water that Antarctic green that water assumes when reflecting a blue sky in a white field. You can see for miles where the Pejar Road meets the road to Crooky. You're atop the Great

Divide on the Upper Lachlan watershed. It's one of the most panoramic views in all New Oireland, as good as that from Paling Yards on the road from Gurnang to Abercrombie or that by the Fullerton turnoff on the road from Laggan to Peelwood.

Thumping out a strenuous three-quarter time on the dash of the ute, I was looking at a certain granite boulder that was making me think of a Mercy nun because of its white coif when I'd a realisation; Dudley Leahy, I scolded, you'll be going the way of this snow and all you can look forward to is that daily single malt for shame on you. Zounds. You take no thought as to why you were chosen as witness and it's not as though you're past it, you just couldn't be arsed. Why, you've scarcely a friend in the district since you opened your gate to a wind farm. Why not tell this tale you need to tell? One won't hurt. Imagine you're being kept alive for a purpose and do your homework.

So I off to the cemetery in the yard of St Stephen's Pejar to get me some perspective. I then rang the gaol for Sister Edmund's number. The new Catholic chaplain, hoyden friend of my daughter Fiona, insisted I first divulge to her the name of my first pet.

When rockies who work in the textile shop
Are returned to the A-wing yard
They must walk the gauntlet of human waste
For rockies do it hard
Stinking of other men's piss and shit
They must stand in the baking sun
As officers won't let them change their clothes
Until the day is done
From taunts and abuse from crims and from screws
They have no place to hide
But is that a tear I see on your cheek
Or did somebody spit in your eye?
Your concern is understandable
I'd say you were well on the way
When sex that smacks of Brazilian wax

71

Is your okay pis aller
Hey hey

*Any cleric who seduces young men or boys or is apprehended in a compromising situa-
tion shall be flogged and lose his tonsure. Thus shorn he shall be disgraced by spitting in
his face, bound in iron chains, given six months lockdown followed by six months segro,
subjected to hard labour, vigils and prayers, forced always to walk in the company of two
others and never again allowed to associate with young men or boys*
St Peter Damian OSB *Liber Gomorrhianus*

There was no snow fell in Goulburn last spring but I've seen a good fall at the
gaol prompt a unanimous armistice. Screws and scumbags, rockies inclusive,
started laughing and throwing snow. A jolly time was had by green and blue.

Sonship

We retain a control over dreams. Night after me resolution methought me on me chook-chaser speeding down a length of causeway with Twomey, also on his chook-chaser, some distance behind. I can't recall the context. Suddenly the causeway narrowed and there was sheer cliff looming on the left and I was looking into a red trench the size of a skip bin only deeper and suspended still on my chook-chaser about to fall. Oh no, I thought, if I go in there, farewell, end of dream! Fear of death prompted immediate intervention. I hit the reset button. I altered my dream's trajectory and *immediately* I was back on the causeway, answering hard questions that had to do with names of bulls I'd bred, being posed me by a woman I didn't recognise but felt I knew, lolling over the bars of another chook-chaser and then I woke; abruptly, because while the scheme of the dream eludes me, I felt I was being invited to note I was so in control of that dream I could vary the plot if I so desired in a split second.

Yet I maintain I was not dreaming the night I saw those red-black wounds on a freshly deceased Father Simon of Cyrene. I shall go to my grave proclaiming it. I do concede they fast disappeared which is plenty weird so I don't discuss them. That Brenda still had a crush on the man I would not doubt. I never mentioned zounds in any conversation with her. I never mentioned them in all the sessions I had over many years with psychs and trauma counsellors seeking to assist me through NLP and CBT and EMDR, all at my own expense, because being old-school I would not admit a weakness, certainly not to Ron Woodham.

My weakness was believing what I'd seen. A prison officer doesn't believe eighty percent of what he sees or ninety percent of what he hears.

For a week or two, as I told Trev Ironside, I could see the scene in vivid detail every time I shut my eyes. I was still in shock. I could see his body, his white hair, zounds, the bumf around his neck, the details of his slot, and shock as a rule fades in time. Not here. I was never the same. Cock-shock. My libido departed and as sex had been the one activity never actually bored me, for a spell I rasped away without enthusiasm, but that wasn't good enough for Brenda as she was a highly-sexed woman and probably still is. She could do better and did. I haven't had sex since she left. I'd have liked to have screwed Ms Ucicky but wouldn't have been able.

I do miss that sense of having no chronological age. Only in sex I realise was I fully concentrated. A man has no age when he fucks. I do miss that sense of inescapable thereby justifiable sin.

When a man is negligent he fears the hour of death; when he approaches God he fears judgement.While a man remains in the knowledge and life of the flesh death terrifies him. But when his knowledge is spiritual and he leads a righteous life his mind is at all hours occupied with memory of future judgement.When he has reached the knowledge of truth after knowledge of Divine mysteries has been aroused in him and hope of the future affirmed then love swallows both that carnal man who like an animal fears to be killed and the man of reason who fears Divine judgment.When he becomes a son he receives the adornments of love instead of being taught by the rod of fear

St Isaac of Nineveh

I discussed zounds in detail with the Black Monks in Rome and mentioned them in passing to Sister Edmund and Rev Trev. No one believes me.

Was it perhaps a *vision* I saw in that premonitory nightmare that had me thinking myself under a collapsed scrum? Was I responding to a call for help? Your old men shall have dreams, your young men shall have visions, says the prophet Joel in the familiar lection, so a vision perhaps. Gaols, because of the DICs and non-consensual sex, are hot-spots for psychics and so acknowledged even by the most hard-bitten of warders. I recall Mumbles' unexpectedly mild reaction when a couple of young Kooris were refusing to go in their slot, complaining they were being pummelled about as they lay in bed.

'Is that that slot old Pendennis topped himself?' mused Mumbles, finger on philtrum. 'I think it is.' So he bad the Koori clever man go up and smoke the slot and do a bit of a stomp and a dance to call on the ghost of Pendennis — we could hear this all over the wing — to wake up to itself and to stop fart-arsing about and to make the most of a freedom so dearly won; advice apparently heeded as the two cellies returned to their slot and reported no further humbuggery.

It would be a dark spot to any psychic, Goulburn. There is a stone tunnel reputedly haunted under Goulburn Courthouse that is still used to bring prisoners to the dock. It's up that tunnel Father Bourke would have been escorted though you'll search in vain to find his trial on Trove. Mum knew an old lady who grew up on Clifford Street and she told Mum how as a girl she'd seen a body gibbeted in front of the courthouse where they used to have the gallows for the public executions. Governor of the day, likely Earl of Belmore, saw it on some official visit and said, 'Take that down, that is an absolute disgrace.' They'd put it up again the minute he left town. Mind you, in 1866 alone we hanged ten bushrangers and shot another thirteen dead as they ranged the nearby bush. We're a bad lot in the Irish New Country.

Having determined to get to the bottom of Father Bourke, I went for a cup of tea and a slice of cake at the Roses café, right next door to the courthouse and within sight up Montague Street of our Gothic Revival St Saviour's Cathedral, with its square sandstone tower housing its twenty-one-hundredweight ring of twelve-plus-one. Plenty of parking thereabouts for Sister Edmund's Micra, which is the blue one with the cardinal-and-myrtle Rabbitohs sticker.

Tell me children what did we see as we walked to the park today
Did we see in a gallows-tree a man whose clothes had rotted away?
And were there crows and currawongs upon his toes and face?
And what was the reason tell me for the poor man's fall from grace
Does anyone know?

Miss he was a highwayman who killed a man for gain
And he's in that cage to caution us we must not do the same

Correct

Tell me children what would we see if we walked to the park today
Would we see the HRMCC with a wall so tall and grey?
The man in the tower has a gun in hand
Can anyone tell me why?

He's there to keep us away Miss lest we sneak up on the sly
He's there to forfend the highwaymen from all who pass them by

Mercy mercy and again mercy

'Shall we sit outside, Sister? Nice in the sun if a bit breezy. What would you like?'

'I'll have a double shot flat white, thanks Dud, and if they've any of that nice pear cake.'

'I'll be back.'

'So. Now.'

'Thanks. That looks grand. You've had snow out Grabby?'

'We have. You can feel it in the wind. Would you rather sit indoors?'

'I'll sit here. Would I see Mt Wayo covered in snow if I drive up to the Rocky Hill War Memorial?'

'You can drive all the way out to Wayo in perfect safety, Sister. So you've retired.'

'Who says? I recently attended a chaplaincy conference in the Gambia. I do a bit of work for Mercy Health. We have lots of elderly sisters needing attention. I do some work for the funeral parlours. I bio in and out of the Big House if Cissy needs a hand as the Reverend Ruth is always taking sick. There have to be two chaplains with the men these days.'

'Yes and you know why that is, don't you.'

'I do. What did you want to see me about Dud?'

'Oh just something I mentioned to you at one point.'

'I didn't think we were here to socialize. I'm not saying you weren't a competent AS but they tell me you'd no time for the blue let alone the green.'

'Oh, don't pass on that kind of crap to me. So you've heard I attend the Anglican Church?'

'I did think you were Catholic as you come from a good Catholic family and I've seen you taking Mass at Our Lady of Fatima in Lagoon Street.'

'I was just a three-timer married to a Tyke. I find I require the blood as well as the body and we get both up the hill. We can boast the best church organ in this country. Our vestments are listed by the National Trust. You should see them. Mothering Sunday rose chasuble embroidered by the Karen People of Burma, red with tongue of fire for Pentecost. As to the good Catholic family, my father was an atheist. I attended state school. The old boy had to be seen at Mass or he wouldn't get fencing work if he weren't.'

'You do know, don't you, there's no such thing as an ex-wife? I hope you fold your arms over your chest as you leave the narthex. You've no right to be taking the Eucharist.'

'Bullshit. Sinners are welcome at the Lord's Table. We get in twenty souls up there ten a.m. Sunday we think we're going well. I doubt they'll throw me out and you know it wasn't my idea to get divorced, but there are no grounds. Brenda just up and left taking half the farm which she on sold to an absentee shepherd. I had Biblical grounds for the divorce but we won't go there. Why should I be punished further? As I heard someone say in the gaol one time, it's just not fair.'

'You do what you think right, Dud. I'm not going to sit here defending the patriarchal church. You know my views there.'

'I do indeed and I think we're singing from the same song sheet, Sister, as we both believe in one Holy Catholic and Apostolic Church. Let's leave it at that. Did I not see you at Mumbles' funeral?'

'You did. Poor Mumbles, without the cap he reminded me of Sam Burgess seen in profile. Can the Rabbitohs make the final eight without Sam?'

'It's way worse than that. They didn't turn up last week. Letting Craig Wing go was the big mistake for mine as he was a genuine utility, but back to Mumbles' funeral, I was standing outside the ex-chapel when I noticed the graves of all the religious, so next day I returned and found the grave of Sister Bridge who died the same day Simon Bourke. You might have told me.'

'Oh pu-lease! You're not going on about Simon again! If you are I'm leaving. Get a grip. You did all right out of Simon, Dud, you got to see the Trevi Fountain. Simon was a rocky who necked himself but one of ours, young Simon. We raised him from a suckling babe. He was one of our grow-your-own slaves.'

'I didn't invent those wounds just to score a trip to Rome.'

'You want my view? You never saw stigmata except in your imagination. We see what we want to. In any event, we don't as yet canonize rockies, preferring to move them. Where did we go wrong with Simon? I wish I knew. He was a dear little boy. I was in the MPU the other day talking to Andrew Garforth who murdered Ebony Simpson up there in Bargo. Jerked off onto her nine-year-old face then drowned her in the dam and freely admits it, so it's no secret. He would have been about in your day. He's now done twenty-two years and like Simon never to be released but SORC gave him a B from an A2 so he could work in industries, which was overturned by the minister after speaking with Commissioner Ray Hadley. You can't tell me it's right they've taken the man's tele. If you haven't the bottle to neck these men, you have to at least allow for the possibility of redemption and that's where you fed us your little bit of berley. How Simon could have done what he did quite beggars belief, but the wonder is someone dogged. Who? As a keen Googler you'll be aware it was kept from the media. No alert for Two Giordano Bruno. You won't find it on the web. We waited for the right judge and we always have the right court reporter here and the right police.'

'And the right coroner and the right zambucks. Well you've three paedophile Christian Brothers from St Pat's up on charges, so someone slipped up. As to Simon there's not much crims don't know and they all told me he was a very very putrid buzzacott. I have the feeling you know what he did but it doesn't really matter if you'd rather not say because as you recall, when I saw that photo of Padre Pio in the Sanctus window in Katoomba Street, and noticed on the Padre's hands the self-same wounds I'd seen on Father Bourke, I had no choice but to conclude that here was a case of redemption. There was a certain creditor which had two debtors, Sister; the one owed him five-hundred pence and the other fifty and when they had nothing to pay, he frankly forgave them both. Tell me therefore, which of them will love him most? To whom little is forgiven the same loveth little. Those wounds were a sign to Corrections but I was the one who saw them. The sign was given me, the baggy Dudley Leahy. I may be heavy of tongue but as to being mistaken, I'd never seen stigmata. I'd never so much as *heard* of stigmata. How could I be mistaken?'

'Oh you're so self-deceiving. No wonder your colleagues couldn't stand a bar of you. He committed suicide! Have you quite forgotten? We've not had Vatican Three last time I checked. As to what you thought you saw, we'd need two witnesses, Matthew 18, and we've only you. That said, you scored yourself a visit to the Trevi Fountain when Mother Borgia passed on what you told me to old Father Mahoney who still lives on the corner of Livingstone Road and Marrickville Road, Marrickville at the Passionist retreat there, what's its name again? St Brigid's, that's right. There never was a St Brigid just as there never was a St Kilda. There *was* a St Catherine McAuley, but being a bit of a horse she couldn't compete with your sultry Mary Mackillop.'

'Oh give us a break. You sound like *Martha* Edmund Quinlivan. Know who else was living at Brigid's retreat house in '94? Only Father Daniel Lyne the notorious Passionist paedophile who'd supposedly left the country like Father Aidan Kay, another Passionist paedophile sent to trial in New Zealand last year for a crime he committed in Hobart. It's all on the Broken Rites website. Passionists disappear them. Well, they're not Robinson Crusoe there. I'm sorry you don't believe me but more for your sake than mine. Should I believe Trev Ironside when he tells me Father Bourke was Sister Bridge's confessor? Is it true he was never defrocked?'

'Oh, hardly worth the effort. You keep calling him 'Father' as though that meant a great deal but it doesn't. He was just a monk-priest. An abbot in a monastery is a little tin god with power to ordain monks but only to minor orders. In the old days there was a clear distinction between choir monks and lay brothers; in a nutshell, the monks did the praying while the brothers did the work. Simon, as an enclosed religious, could celebrate Mass at Marys Mount but outside that retreat he could only hear confession. Passionists, being too tired to do any work of any kind, are only too happy to sit on the rusty dusty hearing confession. As mere women we Mercy Sisters had to suffer the parish priest come in from OLAF North Goulburn when that was a separate parish to Mary Queen of Apostles to conduct Mass, and a Passionist monk, when there was a Passionist monk, to hear confession. Men were free to enter our convent but we weren't free to enter theirs. Simon would have been Bridget's confessor when he was last man standing as he'd done thirteen years by the time he necked himself. He was Mercy confessor in '69. Bridget was a postulant when he was her confessor, as he transferred to the Big House when the monastery closed.'

'And the statues came over the river. What was his crime, Sister? Be frank. I think you owe me that. Give me understanding and I shall live.'

'I owe you nothing. Get it straight. Those statues were only on loan to us, Dud. When we shut up shop the Passionists took them back and they're now in the Adelaide Hills.'

'They weren't theirs to take! Jesus, Mary and Joseph that's a sore point round Crooky but we won't go there because those statues were purchased by subscription from local families to commemorate deceased loved ones. Now listen: I want to know what happened the day Bridget Poidevin died. I want to know how she died and I want to know where. You *do* owe me that. You do owe me that because I told you what I saw in Katoomba Street in good faith and it was meant to be confidential and as to that bloody Trevi fountain, I wish I'd never mentioned it. It wasn't half as good as I made out.'

'Fetch me another coffee and cake, I'll see if I remember. I'm doing you a favour now, Dud.'

'Oh you're always doing me favours Sister Edmund.'

'It's a shame we lost our Begonia House over the road. Have to go to Bathurst now to see a decent begonia.'

'That can be arranged. I'll take you up to see the Begonia House in Machattie Park.'

'I can't be seen in a car with a divorced man.'

'Well then I'll hire a van with tinted windows.'

'Look at the tan on that girl. My goodness.'

'That's not a tan, Love. That's a tandoori.'

    Temptations is the restaurant

    Flamingos is the nite-spot

    Distractions is the gaming room with pokies by the score

    We thank the Lord for Foxtel

    We thank the Lord for whisky

    We thank the Lord we don't look forward to answering the doorbell any

                                         more

A shocking thing entirely

'She went to work early that day. What day of the week was it?'

'Tuesday.'

'Tuesday. She would walk to the gaol via Kinghorn and Chatsbury onto Maud. Less than a klick. Barefoot.'

'Dead-set. And would she always wear traditional garb?'

'Always. Discalced feet, shaven head, always watching and fasting. I've seen the stripes on her arms and legs where she used to flog herself. She had the loveliest of red hair and shaved it off. Mother Borgia was none too keen on the traditional garb but it cast a spell over the scumbags. Not surprising: in the Irish south window at St Patrick's church Boorowa, St Brigid is depicted as a nun in Mercy habit with halo holding a Lenten candle, though we didn't worship at St Pat's in my day. We worshipped over the road at our own chapel dedicated to the Sacred Heart. We had a convent in Boorowa from 1882 till 1994 where I spent many a year after Signadou in Canberra teaching at St Joseph's School. I left in 1980 when the first lay principal appeared.'

'You wouldn't approve that. You know I had a notion you were mostly up at St John's Orphanage here, foolish me. I'll tell you this: Bridget Poidevin was ahead of her time. When you're far enough behind your time you're actually ahead of it. I read where the Dominican Sisters of St Cecilia in Nashville Tennessee, one of the few convents still attracting Western postulants, wear traditional garb even when playing basketball and follow strict observance. Would Bridget have had any trouble getting hold of traditional garb?'

'Goodness, we've a bad web habit haven't we, Dudley Leahy. No our cupboards are full of it.'

'I see you favour the Hillary Clinton pants suit these days Sister, but you keep the name Edmund. Why is that?'

'Convenience. It is the name I am known by.'

'And where did she hail from, this Bridget Poidevin?'

'Limerick.'

'Ah well that accounts for it. A Viking town reminded me of Tralee, a nasty place. McCourt smashed it in Angela's Ashes. Not too many tourists visit Limerick. All the men have bad teeth as though they're on the 'done which well they may be. I was travelling on Bus Eireann from Galway to Killarney once and stopped off in Limerick and got in a fight in a pub over whether prawns are fish.'

'I'm speaking of our local Limerick Dud, just past Phils River on the Peelwood Road. All there is now is that corrugated church which has the power connected still and I believe they still hold meetings in the little annexe but it's been a while since they held a service at Saint Fiacre's.'

'You mean she affected the accent?'

'It seemed native to her. They're an inbred lot out Limerick. Many a pastoral family there spoke Irish when I was a girl. All as poor as church-mice, rarely ventured as far afield as Laggan let alone Crooky. Shearers. Bridget was the youngest of thirteen children all of whom survived.'

'Good Lord. So they made their own entertainment.'

'They had to. How many children have you?'

'Four but I don't see much of the eldest three. They took their mother's side after the divorce and don't feel a need to cultivate goodwill. It takes them a week to respond to a text. Mind you, they can afford to do that because I have to leave them an equal share of my estate. If I don't they'll take it to court and the lawyers will cream the lot. Legals come out of an estate. How convenient. Was a time you got a show of respect in your old age as you had power to make a binding will.'

'Oh this world without religion, Dudley, what a dreadful place. What a shocking thing this same sex in Ireland! A defeat for humanity, says the Vatican Secretary though no comment from our Jesuit Pope. Sodomy, which St Peter Canisius aces in describing as the never-sufficiently-execrated depravity, is the greatest sin of all according to St Bernadine of Sienna, yet I recently read where sodomy is actually very healthful in virtue of its stimulation of the prostate gland. I should have thought paedophilia the worst of all sodomy but that said, I'm only a female knuckle-dragger. What would I know? I'm told things have changed. Have they? Psalm Nineteen assures me the judgements of the Lord are unchanging and righteous every one. You won't see too many same-sex couples with thirteen children. No wonder the Irish turn from the Church when the Pope can say of a poofter priest who am I to judge? Judge not lest ye be judged, yes but St Maximus the Confessor observes that while he who loves God cannot but love every man as himself, the passions of those who are not yet purified find no favour with him. Well our Argentine Pope is on the back foot to the

LGBTIQ and aren't we all. They held their Sydney Mardi Gras on a Saturday in Lent. Can't even translate Mardi Gras. I wonder what they've in common when the L's are L because they hate men and the G's are G because they fear women. When last in Dublin I saw the Pantibar, that's that gay bar run by the drag queen from Ballinrobe, what's her name again? Panti Bliss that's right. Panti Bliss. I ask you. It was Panti gave the famous speech at the Abbey and led the Yes campaign by pointing out that any Irish arsehole can get married. It was Panti embraced by the rogue Gerry Adams at Dublin Castle the day after the refo and to think she hails from Ballinrobe, which is close by Knock in Mayo. We Mercy Sisters first came to Goulburn from County Mayo and this a full twenty years before the apparition of St Mary seen in the company of St Joseph and St John. I'll cut to the chase. Bridget went early that day to the gaol but was back by breakfast. She didn't take it. She went to the garden and knelt in front of the Fourth Station of the Cross. I'm only repeating what Mother Borgia told me.'

'The Fourth Station you say. Well I reckon she must have seen or heard the ambulance on its way to the gaol and put two and two together. I'm told by Trev Ironside she spent a lot of time in his slot with Father Bourke which would have upset the entire gaol, given the regard in which she was held by green and blue alike. I understand Bourke never spoke in thirteen years but he was seen talking to her.'

'I went to work and when I returned Mother Borgia told me she'd hot-wired the caretaker's ute, a '74 HQ Belmont.'

'Oh she could drive?'

'Heavy vehicle license. Farm girl. Rolled it in the gravel outside Limerick. Probably swerved to avoid a roo as she was very fond of animals and got her feet tangled. Still wearing full kit. Did you never see a Cistercian monk trying to sit at an organ stool? Killed on impact, wrapped it round a tree. Go too hard and you bend it. We asked for her body to be taken to St John of God Hospital before that became the Bourke Street Health Centre and for all involved to respect our need for privacy so the matter was never made public. You won't find it on Trove.'

'I didn't. Well thanks for your candour, Sister.'

'Oh I'm dismissed now, am I? I replaced her as chaplain.'

'You did your best. As to same sex in Ireland, what price our Land of Saints and Scholars?'

'That was a world of miracles, Dud. We don't get them now.'

'I'm not so sure. Any query I pose I would have the answer within a split second if we'd decent broadband out Grabby.'

'Google won't give you the answer regarding Simon Bourke and I wouldn't believe prison gossip there if I were you. As to me, my lips are sealed. I hope I make that clear. Thanks for the coffee. What did you think of that escape from the MPU the other day? It was done in broad daylight and he had to have climbed the wall in full view of McDonald's carpark.'

'They'd have been cheering over their Big Macs. You can blame it on Ron Woodham. As a cost-cutting measure we've had no sentries in those northern towers for many a year.'

'He had to have cut his way out of his yard.'

'Yes well he'd a hacksaw blade he knocked off from the carpentry shop.'

'Either that or someone brought it in in the hairy handbag.'

They say everything can be replaced
They say every distance is not near
So I remember every face
Of every man who put me here
I see my light come shining
From the west down to the east
Any day now any day now
I shall be released

Bob Dylan? Certainly worthy of a Nobel Prize, utterly bogus, got to be Bob who should stick to his Frank Sinatra songbook. Found by the G-block photocopier

Thirty thousand piglets

Thought I best take a look at our local Limerick so after my tete-a-tete with Sister Edmund I drove all the way out to Tuena then back to the Sapphire Country through Binda. It's been a while since I saw Tuena as I don't like fossicking mullock and I drive to Bathurst via Taralga since they sealed the Tableland Way. Saw a mob of feral swine running along a fence line in broad daylight out Mt Costigan. The pigs were black, the sounder, maybe thirty sows and piglets pink. Unsealed road, dead roo or wombat in varying stages of decomposition every hundred metres, the wombats mostly supine, the roos with their paws in that futile supplication. Had I been riding the chook-chaser my nostrils would have trembled from the stench of marsupial meat.

I cull roos for dog meat and rabbits for the cat. On my place an abandoned carcase is quickly consumed as I have a feral pig problem thanks to my hobby-farm neighbour. He's the fool who slashes his bitou bush with his little Massy-Ferguson. He'll be getting a good crop of bitou next year, it'll spring up horrent as the hair on a cat's back. Pigs get onto my place through the wombat holes under the fence. The wombats are heavy breathers like those hot-air balloons you see over Lake Burley Griffin on still winter mornings and go right through any netting ignoring a hot wire. Should I go out spotlighting roos I'm only providing meat for pigs. They're meat-eaters. I left them some grain, they wouldn't go near it, wouldn't touch the grain. One particular varmint not content with skinning roos eats the ribs and pelvic bones as well as the worm-riddled meat. You wouldn't want a fall in front of that lad. Some of them bone out at nearly two-hundred kilos.

The fane of St Fiacre, says the board, was opened in 1912 by Bishop John Gallagher, our Derry-born second Irish bishop. Not a lot to be seen in the untended yard where sheep may safely graze, while the church itself, a small affair of corrugated iron, is in no imminent danger of gentrification. Three wooden crosses still in situ, cream-painted walls with a green roof and six gothic lancet windows all painted opaque blue, the whole on stumps with a flounce of chicken wire designed to keep out rabbits, hasn't succeeded. Mandatory wooden loo under Monterey pine in the rear corner, everywhere sheep shit and pinecones, cement-rendered water tank not being fed by rusted gutters choked with pine needles. This is where she would have worshipped, young Bridget Poidevin. This is where she would have been confessed if not confirmed. She was born in '56, being thirty years old when she died, according to Rev Trev who would have gotten that from Sister Edmund.

Bloody old bitch won't tell me what she knows. What do you do?

I sit on the concrete steps under the door with no handle, listening to the wind in the pines, the lambing sheep, the caw of the raven. There is snow on the ground in places still and in the distance I can see a couple of weatherboard Federation homes clearly abandoned. I rather fancy Bridget Poidevin growing up in one of them as I sense her presence.

Engulfed in blackberries all but the lipstick maple. The windows smashed like those in the Marian College downtown but brick chimney sound as the silver mine chimney at Peelwood. Rusting corrugated iron roof in characteristic patchwork of red and grey, unpruned lichen-clad orchard amid the usual rusting red wire and grey weathered hardwood, relating to chickens, toilets, cow bales, all half blown down, wind-scattered.

The whole gaol being in love with the girl, it had to end badly. You're not a million miles from a convent in a gaol. Both involve physical claustration. You live in cells, you're governed by bells. I once prior to successing the owner confiscated a book called *We're All Doing Time* by Bo Lozoff, which was hollowed out and contained traces of a white powder, but I read in what remained that Bo's Prison Ashram Project, undertaken under the guidance of Baba Ram Someone-or-Other, worked on the premise that boob may become an adventitious convent. In prison as in convent freedoms and choices are withdrawn. People cannot choose what they'll eat, what clothes they'll wear, what work they'll do, what time they'll wake, who'll sleep in the next slot, who'll have sex with them next.

As well as God's forgiveness Bourke would have needed his victim's pardon. So we must find his victim but that's a job for 'ron.

LGBTIQ they are coming for me and they're coming for you and let us not pretend the occasion is one for civilized debate. It is cause for war.

Those who never sought her will be wondering why an oratory
Given to her worship would be sitting in a clearing
That is nothing but an oratory a guesthouse and a garden
And a cell in which Fiacre can remove himself from view
Many seeking knowledge will be lodging in the guesthouse
Gathered at the table for some herbal conversation
Though there won't be any women as they constitute distraction
While the supper will be sugar beet with swede and apple stew
Some in search of solace will be helping in the garden
Hoping that Fiacre may provide some explanation
As to what's become of Jesus with His Holy Ghost and Father
For the focus is on Mary who is wearing white and blue
And the model for her statue and the subject of her portrait
Can have only been a woman though just quietly entre nous
She's a woman like no other as she never has a mother
Or a sister just a brother and that brother could be you

He flees to Gaul for solitude this patron saint of gardeners
And scarcely eats the vegetables he spends his days attending
But feeds them to the poor or to the pigs
The merest morsel satiates the hermit from Kilkenny
Destined to be pestered though all women he eschews
Through love of Virgin Mary while his herbal skills betray him
And his relics will be visited by Richelieu no less
In search of cure for haemorrhoids or St Fiacre's figs

Too easy

I was half thinking of taking a drive through the granite country beyond the Lachlan via Rugby to see the fields of rape in their early flower as when they combine with black wattle in its golden glory on the hills, there's a sight to cool the eye. You do need to dodge the turtles on the Lachlan Valley Way as they cross the road this time of year, the snake-headed turtles. Instead I rang Trev Ironside asking if he'd time to shoot the breeze as being still on tilt I needed to talk.

Trev bought the old rectory that overlooks Taralga town, in particular the heritage-listed bluestone Anglican Church of St Luke's where Trev was never rector. There *was* a rector in the rectory as recently as 2008 but nowadays the entire parish, an early Anglican stronghold in the Irish New Country established in 1838 at Richlands towards Wombeyan Caves as a Macarthur outstation a day's ride from Camden Park and suitable for growing tobacco, is overseen by the venerable Archdeacon of Canberra and the Southern Tableland, who lives in Braidwood and who'd be a busy man in terms of the driving he would need to do if not of the tables he would need to lay.

Trev's billiard room commands a panorama through floor-to-ceiling double-glazer and there are few views I more enjoy though Trev would maintain the fifty-one freshly erected wind turbines on the one-hundred-and-six-megawatt Banco Santander wind farm on nearby Bannaby Road, which now command the northern horizon, introduce a jarring and unwelcome visual note. I can only say they don't faze me and as to the furphy they are bad for health, why I've a mill not two-hundred metres from my back door.

There's a low mournful note from the stem, a bit of switch action, a bit of a whirr as they stop and start, which they will depending on wind speed, but the three big blades just go whish whish whish in an upward manner with a couple of seconds between each whish.

Oh I do wish Trev would take that bloody sleeper from his ear and now he's wearing two big signet rings and a gold bracelet.

'I see you've got some solar panels on your roof there Trev.'

'Yes. I wasn't sure whether to fix them landscape or portrait but went for portrait.'

'Will you give me a handicap?'

'No. We're not playing for a sheep station.'

'Very well. Here I go in off. How's your book coming along?'

'Don't mention it. If you drive up to Berkelouw's Book Barn on the old Hume at Berrima and look in the Religion section you'll find it pretty well-stocked and seldom visited.'

'Yes but your take on Saint Luke, just from what you've told me, will open a few eyes. Hand me the chalk.'

'I used to think that. Now I'm not so sure, though I have to do something on rainy days as Maggie's always in at Anglicare. Oh dear the ball's off the table. I've tried that shot I don't know how many times.'

'Can we talk about Simon Bourke?'

'Simon Bourke. Was he the lad who bronzed up his slot? I can still smell it.'

'No sweeper or baggy would clean that slot. We had to get in a forensic decontamination firm at a cost of seven grand. No, he was the priest who necked himself in A-wing.'

'You've lost me.'

'Come on. I was in your office looking for Sister Bridge who never did submit her DIC report.'

'Was that your first day?'

'Pretty close. You know why she never submitted her report?'

'Because she died in a car accident.'

'Oh. Someone told you.'

'Sister Edmund.'

'Had you much to do with Sister Edmund?'

'We used to work out of the same office.'

'Did she mention to you his, ah, wounds?'

'Wounds?'

'Zounds. His wounds. I told you I saw deep wounds that disappeared on Bourke's hands and feet and would have sworn to it, in fact did, at Passionist headquarters. I know I told you that. I'm surprised you don't recall. Bourke was a Passionist priest from Marys Mount and still a Passionist priest at the time of his decease. It was actually you told me they never defrocked him. Did he commit suicide? Had he made a sexual miscalculation? Was he murdered? These are some questions I seek to resolve. Could I borrow your book on Padre Pio, the one you bought from the Capuchin Friars in Jersey Road Plumpton? Do you still have it?'

'I do. Apropos of Pio, they reckon it was carbolic acid the good padre poured in his hands and feet. I try to put those years in the gaol behind me, Dud. The dumping ground of the clerical world, says Taft in '78, and to think I once thought I could make bishop, if only Bishop of Grafton. I'll get you the book after the game. You can keep it.'

'I think you'd have made a good bishop. I think the Copts have it right there, they elect their pope through sortilege. It's a funny thing Trev, but I can find no mention of Father Bourke and I have searched the web, I have gone through Trove, all the newspapers in the National Library, all the microfiche and I can find nothing. And no one will tell me a thing. It's as though he never existed.'

'Wait a bit. Simon Bourke. It's coming back. You should have searched his case file.'

'I couldn't find it. I couldn't find the coroner's report. There has to have been an autopsy if not an actual inquest but I'm guessing it was a whitewash. Do you know anything about him?'

'Chaplaincy like Justice Health is not part of CS. It wouldn't do for a chaplain to go rummaging through case files. I was never interested in a man's criminal past.'

'I heard him described as very very putrid and you know what that means. He was a buzzacott. What did Sister Edmund say?'

'I can't go into these confidential matters with you I'm afraid. Why are you so interested after all these years?'

'Because of zounds. Here's a priest never to be released and where's the outcry? Where's the victim's family at the Royal Commission?'

'Maybe there was none. When did that home for orphans close?'

'I know what you're thinking. Seventy-eight in the case of St John's, five years after he was gaoled, the year the monastery closed. He was twenty-nine. From talking to officers like old Costello I know he'd done thirteen years which makes him forty-two at the time of his demise and yes, I conclude his victim had to have been an orphan. The girls' orphanage closed in seventy-three and Bourke was confessor at both St John's and St Joseph's from the time he was ordained, which would have been what, sixty-eight? All those orphans were supposedly five to sixteen years but I know they took them as young as three at St John's and sometimes younger. Bourke himself was a suckling babe from St John's Orphanage.'

'Who told you that?'

'Sister Edmund.'

'Well they've kept it in house. It's a Catholic cover-up. Rather strange it went to court. No mention at the Royal Commission?'

'No. And do you know I can find no mention of his trial in any court record.'

'Let it not be said the man in the white zucchetto is losing his touch in Goulburn. It's a Catholic cover-up. Looks to me this game is evenly poised.'

'What did you think of your man Simon Bourke? Come on! It was you told me he was never defrocked!'

'Oh that would have come from Sister Edmund. I don't think I ever saw him. Heard he was always in tears. Never saw him in the yard.'

'So was he always one-out?'

'Wouldn't know.'

'If he was, it's a privilege. He was one-out when he died so he was getting special treatment. I'd have to say his corpse had all the hallmarks of the choke and stroke. I've seen a few gone wrong. The rope, which didn't need padding as it was only bumf, was tied to the tap. He only had to stand to reverse the neck compression but the risk adds to the thrill, so I'm told. Sorry Trev, but I need to talk. I've kept it to myself too long and it's taken a toll. There was spunk all over the floor of his slot. You never saw so much spunk.'

'No, I probably never did. Give us a break! He may have lost control there because of Sister Bridge. She was a right little stunner. I did hear rumours.'

'Oh?'

'I can't repeat them. She may have spent too much time in his slot, which was ill-judged.'

'So you won't tell me what you heard?'

'No.'

'Give us that book on Padre Pio, I'll be off.'

'Oh don't be such a girl. Let's go for a walk, Dud. There's something I want you to see.'

When God plays a game of billiards
He just hits the ball with His cue
And in accordance with the laws of physics
It goes precisely where He wants it to
So He never plays more than a frame and a half
Before retiring to His throne
He can't see the point in billiards
Or anything else if the truth be known

Old people dead finish whole lot

St Luke's with ancillary concrete tennis court and hideous Memorial Hall with Beefmaster barbeque.

'Do they still hold services here?'

'They do. Ah what a day Dud, wouldn't be dead for quids. Blue pacific and hawthorn flowering, willow greening up. I can hear bees. Do you still keep them? It's an authentic country town. Peaceful too, if you don't have a team of motorbikes riding through looking forward to the big sweepers other side of the Abercrombie or a convoy of four-wheel drives heading off to Swallowtail Pass. Great place for a stroll. Listen to those sparrows and white cockatoos! There are sheep lambing in the paddocks that run right through town. Of course, most anything you need, you need to drive to Goulburn. Have you seen our church? I mean our Heritage-listed Celtic Romanesque job? Used to be the first building you saw as you drove over the crest. That was before the wind farm.'

'Is that smoke coming from the convent chimney?'

'It is. Sister Bernadette lives there. Got the place to herself. If it's wet you see her washing line on the upper verandah. Her little car will be out back next to the satellite dish. Plastic bins, gas bottles, all the signs of life but the school next door is closed and the presbytery has no resident priest. Dermid MacDermott comes out from OLAF for Saturday Vigil. In we go.'

'It's the same style of convent you see in Boorowa.'

'They're all the same, mate. And they're all empty.'

I hear a few trapped flies. For a moment I'm thinking, can I get rid of those?

'What do you think? Altar, pulpit and reredos are all Wombeyan Rose marble with the beautiful creamy vein. You won't see it anywhere else except in the tomb of St Mary of the Cross Mackillop, Mount Street North Sydney, because whoever mined it kept it solely for ecclesiastical purpose and the quarry is now closed as part of the Wombeyan Karst Reserve.'

'I think I've been here before. I think I once attended a wedding here, one of Brenda's nieces.'

'There was a stink four years back when the silky oak altar rail was disappeared.

Father McDermott explained it was obstructing coffins during funerals. Thing is, it was donated by the Moodys of Taralga Hotel. The entire building was constructed by donation after the Great Depression. See that photo? That's the first parish priest, Monsignor Austin O'Connor, looking pretty pleased with himself, and why not? Never would Austin have imagined that a mere eighty years on his church would be struggling to fill half a pew, the presbytery next door deserted, the Sacred Heart School closed and St Joey's Convent breathing its last.'

'And why is that do you suppose?'

'Because to everything there is a season. Now here's the window I wanted you to see. It's a strange choice. The big rose window with the sacred heart dates from the nineteen-thirties but the altar and pulpit from the nineteen-forties, except for the little altar facing the nave, which is of course post-conciliar and a sore point with our SSPX out on the Braidwood Road, speaking of which, here he is, the man himself, SPX, first window to your left. St Pious the Tenth. The pope who gave the paedophile priest the all-clear in making weekly confession compulsory from age seven. Have you had any sexual thoughts at all this week my child? Do tell.'

Knuckle-dragger SPX out of shape and unsmiling. Photos exist.

Next past the Lady chapel, knuckle-dragger St Patrick, of whom we have no photos, bearded in bishop's mitre with in his right hand his shepherd's crook and in his left, not so much his pint-sized Armagh Cathedral as in Boorowa, but a single-steepled job over the motto 'St Patrick keep the light of the true faith ever brightly burning in the hearts of our people.'

Christ the King.

And His consort, Our Lady Help of Christians, on the distaff by the side altar of St Bernadette of Lourdes, fourteen-year old peasant girl captured in trans-port of hearing the little lady of her apparition saying 'I am the immaculate conception' which words are inscribed over the altar.

'Check out the blonde Virgin Dud. Check out the red hair on her babe as in the Book of Kells where the Christ child is depicted as a red-haired leprechaun with two left feet. That is apparently the first depiction of Virgin and Child in

European art and it's ugly as a hatful of arseholes yet no one could doubt the illuminator's skill in virtue of his border ornamentations. A very Irish district this, with a big Hibernian Society.'

Moving back towards the narthex now, the Little Flower, St Therese of Lisieux, 'the greatest saint of modern times' (SPX) whose many devotees include Jack Kerouac and Padre Pio, holding roses over the motto 'after my death I will make a shower of roses to fall. I will spend my heaven in doing good on earth'. She is thus twice represented here with window and statuette both. Discalced Carmelite nun died of consumption aged twenty-four and of whom we have photos.

'Here is the window. All these side windows date from the reign of Father Bede Mcphillips in the nineteen-sixties. SPX didn't receive his halo till the nineteen-fifties. The whole church was put together piecemeal and wasn't actually finished till people stopped coming, not wanting to confess to contraception.'

St Maria Goretti is youthful, swarthy, pink-and-red halo, smiling, holding three lilies and standing on a hill of red roses and yellow daisies over the motto 'Why is thy apparel red and thy garments like theirs that tread in the wine press?'

'Isaiah sixty-three, two, Dud. Wherefore *art thou* red in thine apparel and thy garments like him that treadeth in the winefat.'

'Huh?'

'Go home and Google. She's a Passionist saint, a virgin martyr murdered aged twelve by a putrid rocky. Interesting choice for Taralga. She gave her killer the knock-back so he shivved her. Took a while to die. I think he was eighteen or twenty and a bit simple. As she lay dying she forgave him and in boob he repented through prayer — through prayer to *her*. Go home and Google. On release he become a Capuchin friar and actually attended her canonization occasioned by his own testimony.'

'Well there's a tale of redemption I needed to hear. Thanks Trev. You've given me heart. But now you want to be rid of me.'

'Go home and Google.'

St Patrick is brought before the King
'You have let yourself down,' he is told
'You were charged to keep the true faith bright
And you've let yourself be rolled
Is there anything you would like to say
Before I kick your arse?
I am after taking that crosier
And putting you out to grass'
'Bring it on' says Patrick
'I'll be glad to be out of the job
I was never Roman Catholic
Like Monsignor Thingamabob
Or SPX. *Bas imnocht o domhan*
Free of this world and rid of fools!
While as to your sex and your same sex sex
You no playa da game you no breaka da rules

The duty of the rooster has been usurped on Willochra by a red wattle bird, which vociferous wretch greets the dawn in a series of hoarse territorial barks, usually transcribed in the bird guides as 'chok chok chok' but to my ears 'sux sux a same sux sux.'

Nail him up

I often return to the Church of Christ the King. It has become my haven. I don't know if Bridget Poidevin worshipped here as Limerick in her youth was part of the old Crookwell parish but Google 'church Laggan' you'll find a holiday rental.

I don't suppose she came here much but I don't feel a stranger.

The only sound is made by flies that get in through the swinging doors. They avoid the web in the left hand of Our Lady in the Lady Chapel.

I light a votive candle to Our Lady Help of Christians, twenty cents, and sit in the second pew under the Stations of the Cross between the stained-glass windows of Our Lady Help of Christians and the Little Flower. Before me an altar of St Bernadette and next to that on the wall, two photographs, one a montage of eleven vocations produced from this now-defunct parish that was once part of the old diocese of North Goulburn; eleven fair-dinkum Christians including three parish priests and eight religious sisters, the priests displayed, need it be said, above the nuns; not bad going for a town of never more than seven-hundred souls. Eleven chaste folk who gave themselves half a chance of salvation presented here as the pride and purpose of the parish: St Isaac of Nineveh affirms there is no such thing as a lay Christian, only priests and monks and nuns and would-be's if they could-be's: *'He who wishes to progress in the virtue of bearing injuries with joy and magnanimity must withdraw from his relatives and become an exile; for one cannot make progress in this virtue in one's birthplace. Only the great and the strong can bear such sufferings in the midst of their relatives — and those alone can do this in whom the world is dead since they no longer hope for any consolation in this life'.* No Mercy Sisters: the women all wear traditional garb as Black Joeys except for one Good Samaritan, Mother Mary Bonaventure Mooney, and all entered the Josephite Congregation at North Goulburn excepting Sister Mary Alacoque Moloney who entered at Perthville, the original Black Joey convent. Goulburn is a daughter-house of Perthville.

It is, however, the larger photo of our one accredited Australian saint that captures the attention: Sister Edmund was maybe right in calling St Mary of the Cross Mackillop 'sultry' for the Oz-born founder of the Brown Joeys is a strikingly beautiful woman who stares directly at the camera with more than a hint of sensuous defiance.

I can't find a single photograph of Bridget Poidevin.

The Wombeyan Rose marble gives me the nexus to Mary Mackillop and in the dome above the Wombeyan Rose reredos is a life-sized crucifixion, stock-standard Renaissance crux-with-corpus, against a blue sky, in which our Suffering King, attended to either side by sorrowing Marys, hangs on his cross, head bent under the sardonic INRI scroll. One cannot help but focus on the deck spikes through his hands and feet, as all three are of a size and shape as would produce the very wounds I saw, or thought I saw, on the hands and discalced feet of Father Simon of Cyrene Bourke. They would also produce the wounds in the photo of St Padre Pio, taken by Father Placido of San Marco in May 1919, that show the stigmata allegedly received by the padre on Friday 20 September 1918 while he was in prayer at the foot of a similar crucifix in the choir of the small old church of St Ann in the Capuchin friary of San Giovanni Rotondo in Apulia. They started out as pinkish spots accompanied by sharp pain but came to him in permanent form and bled at San Giovanni Rotondo.

They had disappeared within ten minutes of his death.

As he appears in the Acts of the First Congress of Studies on his Spirituality, the book I borrowed from Trev, St Padre Pio was a humble peasant like St Bernadette of Lourdes, a confessor as distinct from preacher, who had this to say concerning the task confronting him:

'Divine pity does not soften them. You cannot attract them with gifts. You cannot tame them with punishments; they become insolent if treated well. They become more evil if treated austerely. They become angry in prosperous times. They despair in adversity. They are deaf blind and insensible to every gentle invitation as to every harsh reproof of divine pity that could shake and convert them. They stay fixed in their hardness and render their darkness more intense. Let me tell you the thought of seeing so many souls who dizzily want to justify their sins in despite of the highest good afflicts me, tortures me, wears out my brain and breaks my heart.'

The First Congress on the Padre's spirituality was held in '72, thirty years prior to his canonization, but that his stigmata can have only been the product of sympathetic imagination is evident from the fact that modern Filipinos who have themselves nailed to a cross come Eastertide, find they must be supported there with ropes, and while they have themselves transfixed with thin modern hardware store nails, they must be cut down before they can do themselves a serious mischief. They don't stay up there long.

Studies on modern cadavers, ceteris paribus, show that deck spikes driven through the palms into the transom merely rend the palms. For an efficacious crucifixion, the spikes must be driven between the bones of the wrists and ditto for the dorsa of the feet.

John Paul the Second, Pluperfect Pope, created four-hundred-and-eighty-two saints, a nice little Vatican money-spinner, given the typical cost to a religious order of putting forward a candidate to the Congregation for the Causes for Saints is half a million euros.

So who paid for Maria Goretti? Given she's a Passionist saint, the Congregation of Discalced Clerks of the Most Holy Cross and Passion of our Lord Jesus Christ, presumably. Yet they'd only the word of the rocky who killed her.

> Stigmata cannot be the gift of Grace
> Unless it be the purpose of our Lord to sanction lies
> To underscore the preaching of his Cross
> Intended to destroy the wisdom of the wise
> Even the common sense of the half-witted
> But given what was foolishness to Corinth
> A stumbling block and heresy to Bethlehem
> That icons have it wrong is no big deal
> We would not want our crux-and-corpus less than more-than-real

Arc up the PPG

I am persuaded there had to have been a Passionist connection for this window of Maria Goretti to have been installed in Christ the King not twenty years after her canonization. She is cited as a Passionist saint on all Catholic websites, though having died a virgin martyr aged twelve, she was never professed. The Passionists claim her through having educated her.

I sit on the silky oak pew under her window. She is patron saint of rape victims. The rocky who shivved her had done twenty-seven years when she appeared to him in a dream, extending him the lilies she holds in the window. On his release he begged forgiveness from her mother and they attended mass together. They also attended together her canonization at the Vatican. It is a tale more to do with him than her. And they believed him and he was just a rocky but they don't believe me and I'm a screw.

We need to know Bourke has been forgiven. So I need to find his victim but first I need to know what he *did*.

The rector of Marys Mount was present, according to website Trove, when Christ the King was blessed and opened by Bishop Barry, but the monastery with most influence over this little pocket of our New Ireland appears to have been the Congregation of the Most Holy Redeemer, CSSR, *Congregatio Sanctissimi Redemptoris*, the Redemptorists from their monastery at Galong in the wheat fields of Harden, now the usual retreat given the few residual brothers and fathers are in their late eighties. The land for St Clement's Monastery, which is a striking sight as you drive in from Moppity, on which the congregation when thriving ran both piggery and dairy, now congeries of empty sheds in the shadow of a three-story brick pile, was donated them by Nick Ryan, ex-con from Tipperary. The entrance board to the abbey says 'Cead Mile Failte.' As distinct from Passionists, whose raison d'etre was prayer and whose symbol the Holy Cross, Redemptorists were preachers devoted to Our Lady of Perpetual Sucker, make that Succour, Siri. Needing a woman's undivided attention, the Christian monk confects for himself an ever-present, unseen virtual woman: more recently, Akiri Uchida has designed three perfect virtual women for the modern Japanese man;

Rinko Kobayakawa, Manaka Takane and Nene Anegasaki, who may be touched only by stylus on portable games console but you can send them email and take them out on dates in real time.

Redemptorists and Passionists did not perdure in the New Ireland. We preferred to settle for the old Eve. As Father Clemente of Santa Maria laments 'what saddened Padre Pio in the last years of his life was the abandonment of ancient traditions by many Capuchins but above all the great decrease in vocations to the Order.'

It is all over red rover, Clem.

By the door of Christ the King is a certificate for the Mission Cross, imprimatur Bishop Barry DD, in remembrance of a mission preached by the Redemptorist Fathers of Galong 28 September 1934, four days before the blessing and opening of the church on the Feast Day of Christ the King, 2 October 1934. The certificate states 'One. A plenary indulgence applicable to the souls in purgatory may be gained by all who after worthy confession and communion shall devoutly visit some church or public chapel and there piously pray for the intentions of the sovereign pontiff and visit this mission cross on the following days; 1 the day of its erection; 2 the anniversary of the day of its erection; 3 the feast of the finding of the Holy Cross May 3; 4 the feast of exaltation of the Holy Cross Sept 14 or on any of the seven following days. Two. An indulgence of five years and five quarantines applicable to the souls in purgatory may be gained once a day on saluting this cross by some external sign of devotion and reciting with at least a contrite heart, one Our Father, one Hail Mary and one Glory Be to the Father.'

I wonder how they kept anyone at Marys Mount, pre-Vatican Two. The horarium was a shocker. Midnight Office, with a novice going around swinging a clacker to wake everyone up, Matins and Lauds followed by an hour of mental prayer, two a.m. back to bed, up at six for Prime and mental prayer, full divine office at all eight canonical hours with several additional periods of mental prayer and meditation. Friday and Saturday fast days. All this in a Goulburn winter. Could you imagine any young man putting his hand up for that today? Could you imagine the outcry were such a regime inflicted on a felon? Yet Marys Mount could boast two-hundred-and-eighty-one professions before it all went pear-shaped in the late nineteen- sixties as I had my arm up to the elbow in a cow's arse.

When fisting a cow you must always use your non-dominant hand. It is the more sensitive. If you've not done it, you'd be surprised how very pleasant it feels though I'm not sure I'd call it sexual pleasure. But then again.

> Pray for the soul of Dudley Leahy
> Pay no heed to what they say
> Pray that his soul be purified
> Of sin he did before he died
> Here was a man who came home drunk
> Here was a man who swore at sheep
> Daughters find that mission cross
> A moment's silence there to keep
> And pray that his soul may find repose
> Ask that the prisoner be released
> Only the quick can heal the dead
> That all this restlessness may cease
> Monster movie boo boo boo
> Monster movie boo boo boo
> Monster movie boo boo boo
> Monster movie a vun and a two

The fury of the highest One is on me and all the waves and tides break over me. Everyone considers me abominable. I must fight and cry alone both day and night. The provincial never talks to me and I don't know why. My confessor scolds me

Padre Pio 19 July 1915

Sapphire country

Fee came out to lunch today bringing the two little girls. She always rigs their hair time-consumingly in plaits. They were beautifully dressed and wonderfully clean. Maybe it's just me, but we love our little children, can't quite get our heads around the filthy way they're made. Fee had been shopping in Bowral so brought out a couple of almond croissants and four chicken-and-leek pies from Gumnut Patisserie. If only we'd pastry cooks like this in Grabby, I said, or even Crooky. Didn't tell her where the almonds came from.

If only we'd a hall like the one in Bundanoon where you can hear on a Saturday morning the likes of Faure's Sicilienne being played by Chinese prodigies from Sydney.

'Thought you preferred the CWA cookbook, Dad. What have you been up to? Cissy tells me you've been chasing after Sister Edmund! Go outside and play girls, I want to talk to Grandpa. See if you can find the little chickens. How are your bees Dad?'

'Yeah not too bad, eh. All queenright. On a clover flow, your mother's salvias, thistle from the neighbour. Might get a bit of Curse this year. Take a jar of honey when you leave and please return the jar. Chalk brood in the puce hive, they'll overcome it. Fungal. Not notifiable. Had to requeen the pink hive but they've brood, five weeks till we see new workers. They'll be ok for next year, touch wood. My two white Wyandottes, Gluck and Glinka are laying in the paddock girls and the ravens have found the nest if I can't. They don't have much to say when stealing eggs. You find the nest Olwyn, you can keep the eggs and I'll give you some money as well and a jar of honey. You didn't see a drill by the front gate Fee? Yellow? My best drill? DeWalt. I've lost it. Hoping Twomey may have borrowed it. Run a bugle into hardwood that drill. Gears Makita could only dream of. American.'

'Don't give the girls money, Dad.'

Fee aggravates me but doesn't mean to. Her sisters aggravate me and mean to.

'Money solves all ills or so we're told. Do you like money, Olwyn?'

'Dad! Just give them a little *time*!'

'There's nothing in my life might interest a little girl.'

'Well it's true they don't drink whisky but Brian and I could do with a bit of help right now. We're moving house.'

'Is that so? I didn't know that.'

'Mum does what she can but she's ill.'

'Yes so I hear. I'd love to see your little girls more often, Fee. Don't get me wrong. I'm only too happy to help. They can come with me tomorrow to Taralga.'

'*Taralga*! What's in *Taralga*?'

'Nothing. I've a friend there that's all, Trev Ironside, used to be Anglican chaplain at the gaol? Rev Trev Ironside?'

'God you're such an aspie. Do we have proper restraints in that ute?'

'Ah. We'll have to stay here.'

'What did you want with Sister Edmund? Nothing to do with Mum I hope?'

'No, just wanted to check something out. There aren't too many of these old girls left, Fiona. We're watching something disappear and it might just be us. No Black Joeys at St Joseph's, a few in retirement next door and of course they're all Brown Joeys since 2012. Speaking of Taralga, the Sacred Heart School in Taralga closed in 2004 and only one Brown Joey left in all Taralga Convent which is Sister Bernadette who'd be a good age. The Goulburn Post says tears were streaming down the kids' faces when they said the last Mass at the Sacred Heart School. Hundred-and-twenty years on the clock.'

'Are you all right, Dad?'

'What do you mean? I've three-hundred white kakadus ripping up my paddocks, is that what you mean?'

'No.'

'Try to scare them with the shotgun but they don't scare easy. All protected vermin know they're protected.'

'Why the Catholic infodump? Why this sudden interest in religion? Why did you start going to church? You wouldn't be hiding something? Did they get it all, Dad?'

'Didn't have to. No it's just my interest in history, Fee. I can't seem to stop myself from staring at Catholic ruins.'

'It's a shame about the fire at the orphanage, or is it? They'll have to demolish the place now surely. Sending us to Joey's was an act of cruelty, Dad. Bloody old bitches those nuns.'

'It was your mother's idea. You weren't sexually interfered with?'

'No. Just bored to death.'

'Sorry to hear it.'

'The minute I hear the words "Jesus Christ" my eyes glaze over.'

'Do they? Well I dare say it's never easy to find the right words.'

'Why do you go to church? You never went to church when we were kids. You're not a real Christian!'

'That's not for a three-timer to say. Never assume you know the state of another person's soul. It's like another person's bad back. One thing I've learned, you wouldn't be here if I'd been a real Christian, Fee. I wonder if you'd say it was a load of rubbish to Cissy. Olwyn doesn't even know who Christ is. I've asked her.'

'Please don't brainwash my daughters. I know why Cissy took the job. It was because there was no one else and she was tired of driving to Queanbeyan.'

'Sister Edmund gave her life to Jesus Christ, Fiona. It must have meant something to her at some stage. She actually married him, which is why she wears that wedding ring.'

'Look! There you go see? My eyes are glazing over.'

My eyes are glazing over at the mention of the Lord

OMG the load of cobblers that we sought to take on board

When we lacked the gall or wherewithal to coax the body forward

To oblivion

She married Brian, a fellow prison officer, at Christ Church West Goulburn, an Anglican church in which neither one had ever set foot. Pair of three-timers. I gave her away but was disconcerted by the choice of reading which she would have gotten from the web. The usual One Corinthians XIII, verses 4 to 8 mistranslated: 'Love is patient and kind. It does not envy or boast. It is not arrogant or rude. It does not insist on its own way. It is not irritable or resentful.' Could only shake my head as Paul is not speaking of Eros but Agape, translated in the King James as Charity, nowadays misunderstood as alms-giving. Charity is incompatible with Eros. Charity suffereth long and is kind; charity envieth not; charity vaunteth not itself, is not puffed up, doth not behave itself unseemly, whereas Eros is jealous, vainglorious, impatient, arrogant, rude and resentful. He delighteth in porn and he faileth.

> Sex is the devil we have to have
> If we seek to keep reproducing
> Father Son and Holy Spirit
> Plus the devil who put us in it

Landscape with portrait

And didn't I spend an unpleasant evening in the TAB at the Gordon under the stag heads of Toohey's New, drinking middies of FourX which they have there on tap, as you wouldn't want be seen drinking whisky at the Gordon unless you were ordering boilermaker Glasgow-style shots with beer chaser. Sat under Jarrod Croker's 2015 Canberra Raiders' Jersey signed by all team members, to view Sky Racing One and Sky Racing Two and Trackside, placed a few bets. Full credit to Jarrod in the headgear, leading points-scorer in the NRL 2015, Jarrod being a distant cousin of Kangaroo and Raiders' utility Jason Croker from Crooky, he being uncle to Raiders' Five-eighth Crooky's Lachlan Croker. There are Crokers everywhere about, they're as common as Carneys. Father Mark Croker was ordained from Taralga Parish in '97 while from the same parish Sister Mary Paulinus Croker from Golspie was professed a Black Joey in '44, the year of my birth. They're both on the board at Christ the King.

I was waiting for a certain Croker to finish shift so I could glean some idea as to where Tosh might be. Eventually in walks your man and possibly thirsty too, as a screw will discard a can of Coke if it's been out of his sight thirty seconds, under the photo of Marilyn Monroe, the quintessential dumb blonde who wasn't really blonde and who certainly wasn't dumb. 'Well' says Croker espying me, 'if it's not Mr Grabben Gullen.' We go back. We both worked on secondment at the Metropolitan Remand and Reception Centre when it opened and they were short-staffed and he appealed my promotion to AS.

'Keep your voice down,' I says with a smile, moving to the stool beside him and leaning upon him slightly as I'm still a pretty big unit: 'When you appealed my appointment to AS you obtained my resume, Croker, which you then used along with the thirteen others you'd acquired, as a handy reference for your own subsequent application, because it was my idea, while acting gate master at Fordwick, to delegate a specific officer to process bail applications, based on my having had to run over the road during lulls in traffic to check the magistrate's compliance on warrant files held in the old Silverwater complex pending relative's bail application, but you took the credit. Yet to my recollection you were in a Hampton pod, no matter mate, glad you made it to AS and as we see SAS, well done. Can we buy you a drink? What are we drinking? I'm inquiring over Tosh. You would recall Tosh? You and he played golf I recall. I'm trying to locate the man.'

'Why would that be, Dud?'

Croker winks at the rest of the bar and gets his expected smirk. That bloody Sister Edmund can't keep anything to herself. She could use her pension pass to get to Bathurst by train.

'Because he knows of a volumizing shampoo for damaged hair that really works.'

Last heard of driving a cab in Queenstown so I drive home with a small win if possibly over the limit.

Never been to New Zealand but haven't had a holiday in years and got top dollar for the weaners, why not? They had a wit in Piggy Muldoon, vituperator fit to rival Keating. I would need to be home over Christmas-New Year as all my neighbours would be away, including my younger brother who'd be water skiing on Wyangala. I'd be pretty much the only person left in all Grabby so I'd be on firewatch and dog-feeding duties. It takes half a day to get round to all those dogs.

It's a destination for young folk, Queenstown, one of those places like Byron Bay on every backpacker's bucket list, so I wouldn't want to be staying in town and queueing for the bus to the bungy jump, but browsing the web I find a ski lodge near Coronet Peak, actually a private residence, very luxurious, out of the way, peaceful, five-star, available November a mere six-fifty a night. I like the idea of the cedar spa where you can swill in naked privacy, staring down at jet boats traversing the Shotover. It's only three hours by Jetstar from Kingsford Smith.

I've a window seat but nothing to see once we clear Botany Bay and head over the ditch. The Land of the Long White Cloud was all rugby to me. At one point I was in the mix for a Wallaby Jersey number three but all I have to show for that are the ears of a Kevin Mealamu.

Farewell to the wine-dark Tasman. We are now moving over middle-earth as if borne off the Orthanc Pinnacle behind Gandalf on the wings of Gwaihir the

Wind-Lord with the peaks of the Misty Mountains, Redhorn, Silvertine, Cloud-yhead, west of Dimrill Dale, entering the world's most scenic and most danger-ous airport approach. We are looking south toward the magic wood of Lothlo-rien, first settled by Silvan Nandorin elves in the First Age and later home to Galadriel, impervious to the evils of Mordor through power of her ring Nenya. A collective gasp as we recognize to starboard of our Airbus A320 the Ford of Bru-inen, only ford over the entire Bruinen River, where Arwen called in the flood in the form of horses to kill the forms of the Ringwraithes and is not that the rise of tussock where camped the Fellowship of the Ring following their loss of Gandalf and where the refugees escaped from Rohan and where Eowyn cooked up the stew while the cabin crew disarmed the doors?

It is almost thirty years since my first night in the Killing Fields so I didn't think he'd be still driving cabs, the old Tosh, but that's him, my quest is over before it's barely began. I recognize the soft freckled cheese of the billowing elbow and he always kept his chin down low towards his sternum as if holding a pillow there ready to fit a slip.

'Hey! You hif to take the first kib!'
'Sorry mate, that driver's an old friend. Don't pack a sad, will this cover it? Tosh! It's me! Dud Leahy! Remember me from Goulburn Gaol?'
'I try to put those yirs in the gaol behind me. Where to?'
'Ah. Let me just put my port in your boot I know: take me to Isengard the fortress of Gondor where Meriadoc Brandybuck and Peregrin Took were made wardens of the door by Treebeard of Fangorn and his Ents. Then I should like to see Amon Hen the Seat of Seeing where Boromir died in battle before a quick look at Ithilien so we could visit the wood where the battle between the Rangers of Gondor and Haradrim mounted on Mumakil was watched by Samwise Gangee and Frodo Baggins from behind a tree. How long would that take?'
'Forty-five minutes. We can't go on to Ithilien without a four-wheel drive. We're talking the other end of this lake.'
'That should give us plenty of time.'
'For what?'
'Talk.'

'Oh no! I won't be drigging over the past! You should kitsch another kib.'

'I didn't come all this way to sit in a hot tub and drink like Frodo, Sam and Pippin at Frodo's house in Crickhollow. They told me at the Gordon I'd find you in Queenstown and by the oath of Feanor and his Seven Sons. . .'

'Speak not to me in words of omen! When hobbit Merry said to King Theoden of Rohan "I will be riddy even if you bid me ride with you on the Paths of the Dead" Theoden replied "Speak not words of omen! For there may be more roads than one that could bear that name."'

'It's no doubt very beautiful Tosh but it does nothing for me. What are we looking at?'

'The Remarkables and Lake Wakatipu. Do you need accommodation? As an Aussie you deserve the beast.'

'No it's all sorted. We're shortly off to Arthur's Point. Tosh, do you recall that priest necked himself in A-wing?'

'No. Are we right to go?'

'Tosh, don't lie. It was my first night in the gaol and Laid-Back Lester locked me in the slot. You had to let me out.'

'Do we have an addriss in Arthur's Point?'

'Listen: I don't give a shit what happened that night mate, murder, suicide, choke and stroke, I'm only here to talk about the state of his body and the *wounds* Tosh, the *wounds*, zounds, those wounds to his hands and feet. The wounds that disappeared. I'm talking those red-black wounds. You didn't mention them in your incident report.'

'I can tell you why. What are you fucking talking about? What do you mean the wounds that disappeared?'

'They were gone by the time you fetched the nine eleven. They were pink splotches when you got back. Yes I know it's plenty weird but you were first to see the body. You were FRO. You were his gaoler in the days prior. You would have seen him in his slot. You *must* remember! You *must* recall those holes in his hands and feet mate, those red-black holes that weren't bleeding. Please. I'm begging you. That's all I want to hear. That's what I need to hear, give me some confirmation for my peace of mind, too late now for official action, why not come clean? I know you left the gaol within the month. Laid-Back Lester is dead.

Stigmata fade within ten minutes, so we're talking stigmata. I actually watched them fade as you fetched the nine eleven. I don't give a shit who knocked him. I don't give a shit who left his slot unlocked.'

'Hey hey hey steady on!'

'Just tell me what he *did*. That's what I need to hear, what had he done to deserve it? You didn't try to resuscitate him, you whistled as you fetched the nine eleven. Was it something to do with Sister Bridge?'

'Arthur's Point addriss please. Did you ever hear her laugh? Did you hear that woman laugh? She was a ray of sunshine.'

'So it *was* to do with Sister Bridge. I thought as much. You fucking grub. You fucking prick I should just *belt* the fucking truth out of you!'

'Won't help. Give me the addriss in Arthur's Point or git out of the kib.'

'Arthur's Track. Seems I wasted my time.'

'We all waste our time, Dudley, until we seek the Lord Jesus. You should put those years in the gaol behind you. Would you visit Milford Sound? Well worth a look. Take a couple of days. Did you book yourself a meal at the Botswana Butchery? Order the slow roasted shoulder of Merino and weep.'

'How's your sex life, Tosh? I lost my marriage because of what we saw and smelt that night.'

'You should have been offered counselling.'

'I was. You still play golf?'

'This is the addriss. Go in peace.'

'To love and serve the Lord. Yes I try.'

'You don't try hard enough. I can't feel the love. You are a sad and lonely unit aren't you Dudley Leahy, and furthermore you are fucked in the head. Where's your credit card? Do you mean to pay the fare?'

'Oh. Sorry.'

Hobbits speak in their rhotic Gloucestershire accent each to each
As they re-enact the bastard saga amidst the bastard beech

The foundation of all good things, the return of the soul from the enemy's prison, the way leading to light and life is contained in the following two methods; fasting and remain-

ing constantly in one place ceaselessly occupied with thought of God. . . If a man neglects these methods he will come to the two contrary vices, namely bodily wandering and dishonourable gluttony

St Isaac of Nineveh

Portrait with landscape

I saw him again next day. Noticed the Landcruiser Prado as I went for a stroll to search for hives. Bees aplenty were seeking moisture from the hot tub cover. The hives were just around the corner next to the road. Three of them brightly paint-ed. As I was walking back Arthur's Track someone bipped the horn. It was him. Just a friendly bip. Duration of bip important, duration of bip *all*-important.

'Thought you might like to visit Ithilien.'

'Oh how thoughtful. I'll settle for a trip into the supermarket as there's nothing to eat in the cupboards.'

'Don't you have iksiss to a vehicle?'

'I do. There's one in the garage I was told I could use but I can't quite open the door. When I hit what I thought was the remote, the lawn sprinklers came on. What's that little bird there with the headgear?'

'Californian quail. So did you contact your agent?'

'Because of the cost of global roaming I didn't bring a phone. Took me quite a while to get into the place. I thought I'd entered the right code. Luckily, the lady over the road helped out.'

'You could always hitch. Not too far.'

'Too ugly and now too old. Too old for this place, mate. Too old for modernity. When I did get in, I was confronted with, I counted them, fourteen remotes. I can't turn off the fan over the stove hood, it's roaring. I can't work out the prompts on the touchscreen for the induction plates. I accidentally brushed the oven with my hand and the oven came on. The remotes along the walkway to the house go on and off all night and there are no light switches. I think I creased a blind where I squeezed by to get onto the deck as I can't work out how to open the curtain.'

'Suck it up Buttercup, as we said in the MPU. And you thought we were a backward people. Let's get you provisioned.'

'Thanks Tosh. Thanks heaps, mate. I know I don't deserve it. I am a fucking mess. You're right. Fancy forgetting my pin! Won't you please come in and help me drink this Pinot?'

'Should just git bick.'

'Please. Let's just see if we can get the stove to work.'

'What about the hot tub for the skiers?'

'You're right. The hot tub works. Let's have some beers in the hot tub. Not supposed to take glass into the tub but I think that would only apply to drunks. Great views from the tub.'

'Ah. Just to be able to watch TV at night you know? I'm so grateful Tosh.'

'Did you come all this way just to watch TV at night? Don't you have TV in Goulburn?'

'We do. I know you don't believe me but I came all this way just to talk to you about the *wounds*. Those wounds that disappeared and no, I'm not fucked in the head.'

'Then you've achieved your ambition and yes, you are fucked in the head.'

'Let's not spoil the reunion. Chin chin. This is not a bad drop. I did think it would be cheaper. There's the jet boat coming back.'

'He was a piece of work, the Reverend Rocky Buzzacott. Remember Abdul the Bulbul? I had him on my patch. His eyes were always saying something different to his mouth. While he was polite and corrickt in what he said his eyes were murderous.'

'You're telling me Bourke was like that?'

'Couldn't look in Bourke's eyes. They drew you to another place.'

'Better or worse?'

'Couldn't say. Never went.'

'Zounds. Come on. Tell me you saw them. I swear to Christ I watched them fade. Were they there the night before?'

'He has fisted and fucked a little boy. Does that answer your question? He has grabbed him a fistful of love. Does that answer your question?'

'You saw his case file?'

'Just what I heard.'

'Don't believe what you hear. Obiter dicta, mate. Scuttlebutt. What happened the night he died? Come on. It's clear to me you must have colluded with Lester in having him knocked.'

'That is the alcohol speaking. Never presume to judge the state of another person's soul and don't believe what you see. Get me those remotes I'll open the garage door.'

'Tosh! *Please!* The *hatred* he must have provoked! What had he done to deserve it?'

'You can work that out. I told you what he'd done. He had grabbed him a fistful of love. I didn't see what you did is all you need to know now get me those remotes. You are fucked in the head did you realize?'

'Bullshit. It was only my first night in the place. I hadn't had time to get fucked in the head.'

The rest of my short stay in Queenstown I pretty much spend in the hot tub, drinking bottles of Burgundy while watching bees alight and depart from the clammy hot tub cover. They would make me think of Edmund Hillary, he being a beekeeper, and he would make me think of Sister Edmund, who like Tosh would not tell me the truth. Luckily, another 'why' now raised its ugly head: why was I so unmoved by all these legendary lakes and peaks?

Because I couldn't see them in Ireland?

Because I couldn't see them in Ireland.

Tosh had become a Christian too, perhaps to assuage conscience. Had there been a force for good emanating from Bourke?

The Passionist Superior-General asked was it possible I'd imagined the whole thing. I'd said no.

As regard Bourke, a man can generate over the course of a life such animosity that when he's murdered the police know they're under no pressure to solve a crime that was never going to be an easy crime to solve. Let's call him Eugene, as that was his name. Furthest thing from a watermelon man who swaggers round the yard with large invisible watermelons held in the crook of each arm, Eugene, a Fairfield boy of Russian extraction, pebble glasses, very bright, showed not the slightest remorse at having stabbed to death a man who had welshed on a drug deal, fair enough, and a woman who was in the room at the time and may well have been involved, who would know, but scandalously and can you believe it, an innocent dog who happened to be asleep on the floor? It was the murder of this innocent dog that so appalled his fellow inmates.

Eugene served his time and was eventually released from Berrima. Dispatched to reside in a housing commission estate on the Central Coast, he antagonized his neighbours for whom he had open contempt, but as he couldn't find work he couldn't afford to move.

One day he took a train to Sydney to visit an art gallery. On his way home late that night he found himself at Strathfield Station awaiting a connection. It appears he took a stroll. His body was found next morning bashed to death a few blocks away. Police conjecture he must have been recognised by someone who hadn't seen him in some time, squeal of tyres, flash of brake lights. Don't suppose it would have been one of his neighbours from the housing estate. Can't envisage any time soon a petition being presented to parliament. You can get away with murder provided you're not caught red-handed and are circumspect in whom you decide to knock.

From the fact they label informants 'dogs' you might think prisoners didn't like dogs. In point of fact they love dogs. They adore dogs.

> The bouncer and the turnkey own the door
> As they control what happens on the floor
> The one determines who will get to vend you happy pills
> The other could arrange that you be cured of all your ills
> Through courtesy of bumf or the component of a bike
> Should you incur the got-to-go from green and blue alike

Erewhon

Jack Duggan's Irish pub in George Street, Bathurst celebrating the Munster-born armed robber has a photo in the bar of the Munster rugby side that beat the touring All Blacks twelve-nil at Thomond Park, Limerick in '78. Some of the lads are all-but bald but some have long hair and Viva Zapata mo. It was an amateur game then. I gravitate to that photo as I don't like drinking with the screws from Bathurst Gaol and am bored by road bowls and dancing at the crossroads.

Visiting Bathurst I always stayed at the Quality Motel, used to be the James Cook, a block from the head of the lion with the key in its mouth on the gate of the gaol. Come twilight, I would order the double rack of lamb and spend a pleasant hour or so sipping craft beers while watching red Finemore semis swinging wide to take the right. There's a Ron Finemore depot in Orange and the Celsius Restaurant overlooks the roundabout where the Midwestern Highway parts company with the Mitchell. I never tire of watching trucks turning round a roundabout.

I didn't see one Tongan face the whole time I was in Queenstown except at the rugby shop by the Botswana Butchery. There was a dedicated pop-up Jonah Lomu channel on Foxtel NZ featuring tributes and endless footage of a youthful Jonah trampling his way downtown. He was a beast. I recall when visiting Munster in 2003 seeing a huge photo of his face on a Cork City hoarding. I can't recall what he was flogging so it didn't have quite the intended effect but it certainly caught my attention. I hadn't seen a non-European face the whole time I was in Munster and the ad was using Jonah's face the way Peter Weir uses David Gulpilil's face in *The Last Wave*.

Suppose the Irish and not the All Blacks were number one side in the world, would they enjoy comparable aura? I recall how Brenda would always want to watch the opening of a Bledesloe match. As soon as the haka was over she would resume what she'd been doing. Her instinct was sound. We turn to art for consolation and the All Blacks are a dance troupe. Yes they can play rugby as well but they're principally a dance troupe. They multi-skill. They dance and while the dance may be short, the dance is no mere preface.

Where else would you see a war dance performed by a platoon of twenty-two men trained for the dance through hard-contact sport and not stretching at the barre? Big-boned Scots and their Polynesian colonized threaten a common foe. It's a post-colonial masque. I can't offhand think of a single great Kiwi film. *The Hobbit?* You'd be looking for dark Irish wit. I thought the Finns had something special, hint of Paul McCartney in Split Enz, touch of Uncle Albert Admiral Halsey in Six Months in a Leaky Boat.

I never had a problem with the Munster landscape as distinct from the NZ landscape. There was always something there for me, always something to inspire. Munster never disappointed. Even an ugly tatty place like Limerick didn't disappoint.

> How shall we level the playing field before the kick-off here?
> We shall turn our backs on their haka with our earplugs in our ear
> Without the war dance they are just another rugby side
> Seeking unfair advantage an advantage now denied

I never got to dance on a football pitch.

There's a sheep station Erewhon in the Rangitata Valley in the Canterbury High Country noted as a Clydesdale stud. In contrast, the station owned by Samuel Butler, author of Erewhon, who spent a mere four years in the Canterbury High Country setting fire to fifty-five thousand acres of black birch, was actually named by Butler Mesopotamia. Surrounded by the Two Thumb Range, it is the site of the city of Edoras, capital city of Rohan, that houses the Golden Hall of Meduseld. It was in that hall that Aragorn, Gimli, Legolas and Gandalf first encountered Theoden, last king of the Second Line of the Royal House of Eorl.

Whithersoever Ithilien

Sister Edmund in the know refusing to divulge while at the same time adjuring me not to believe yard gossip. Yard gossip tending towards the fisting and fucking of a two-year old boy. Could you actually fist a two-year old? I have disembogued a few victims of the celly's fist to Justice Health and they were grown men. Nasty wounds, bound to become infected. Concerning the in-house incident that led to Bourke being knocked, the Rev Trev would not divulge rumours he'd heard concerning Sister Bridge, while Tosh was indisposed to concede he'd left the slot unlocked. I had been told by a segro desperate Sister Bridge had let herself down, which could only mean sex. As to whether I'd actually seen what I thought I saw, who knows. There are days I doubt it. It would be a cruel delusion that grew more intense as the years passed, which is not to say it may not have been in the end a religious vision. The religious visionary is anyway treated with respect in the Catholic faith, as witness the shrines of St Bernadette of Lourdes and St Margaret Mary Alocoque at Christ the King.

Does anyone really think they actually saw what they said they did?

A year had now passed and Brenda had died but nothing much else had happened. I was just doing what had to be done, trying to get drunk in the evening (a remissible vice). At three a.m. I'd wake in a sweat thinking, why am I still here?

But we *do* turn to art for inspiration so I felt I needed to seek out the art that may have inspired both Bourke and Sister Bridge, which I knew where to find. I always think of that pair in connection with the Stations of the Cross. It would be less arduous than trying to interrogate folk who won't talk. There was a time a contumacious felon who stood mute in the dock was pressed to death under heavy weights in the torture of Peine forte et dure. If you died without plea your property would not escheat to the crown. And one thing you learn guest of the governor, you can't be sure you are getting the truth from a felon even if you fustigate him. He'll only tell you what it is he thinks you want to hear.

So you've got to think laterally. You've got to use intuition.

That August I flew to the City of Churches to revisit the Stations of the Cross

I hadn't seen since I had my one live sighting of Bourke in the garden of Marys Mount.

> You tell me you've no tolerance for any kind of art
> Yet you always find the time to watch a war dance
> At the Bachelors' and Spinsters' if a spinster wins your heart
> And you haven't got the moves you know you've no chance
> You will always watch a movie if there's nothing else to do
> While you're polishing the car I've heard you hum a tune or two
> And I doubt you'd go to church at all to grace the wooden pew
> Were your Saviour there depicted as a Middle Eastern Jew

Ah t'ats grand

I'm in Ireland. Last week of October just drove south to Lake Bathurst to see the rape in juxtaposition with the Curse, orpiment with indigo straight from the Book of Kells. South Hill is covered in Patterson's Curse and even my bees have a bit to work in the old horse paddock. As you drive from Garroorigang to Lake Bathurst you see quite a few fields of flowering rape round Inveralochy. I can't believe how green it all looks in this late wet spring we've just had. To see the low mist and cloud on the hills, the deciduous street trees in bright early leaf puts us all in a good mood. We say it's because the only problem we have right now is scouring but it's more because we think we're back in the Old Country that is really the New Country because this is the Old Country. The Irish New Country is the Irish Old Country. Australia geologically is far older than Ireland and there were people along the Mulwaree millennia before there were people in Athlone.

Early September I drive on impulse to Bathurst though I've been up since four –thirty, which is when an English blackbird starts to sing outside my window knowing he has my undivided attention for half an hour. I go to church first. Another fifty mm of rain on a thoroughly rain-soaked earth has created the perfect New Ireland. Never saw I the countryside look so well so early with the cattle price so firm, never saw I the first fronds of the Chinese toon so pink. I grow forage brassica for the liquorice all-sorts and am so glad I don't have to sit on the verandah nursing a whisky as I ponder whether I'll be able to get the header on if the rain don't ease. Hearts out to Cowra, it's always your best harvest you can't get off. My only crop at present is asparagus planted by Dad and, chooks on the lay, I'm eating asparagus omelette, best tucker of the year. The hills and slopes are emerald green, the wattles in late flower with the little violet creeping pea false sarsaparilla brightening the banks. Lots of early white and pink blossom in the prunus, not that bees will work. Nine degrees max, a caution for snow and ice at Black Springs and grey sky with patches of showery rain on the blue hills, yet I know that in the last light that low will yield to a high and sunlight angle in from under the cloud. So after a scoffee at the Kelso Caltex I drive straight back to enjoy the chiaroscuro. I am close to feeling love for my household gods in this North Atlantic light. The endless refrain it's not Ireland, it can't be real, it's not

Ireland, it can't be real, tends to fade. The knowledge I'm still in North South West does act as a dampener. I have no local history. Yes there were people here forty thousand years before Munster but we're talking history not prehistory and civilisation, as William Faulkner attests, begins with distillation. The Neolithic Revolution was driven by the need to provide a reliable alcohol source. Bread was a by-product.

All the streams are in spate spilling into the basket willow, the Wollondilly by the gaol, the Little River at Porter's Retreat, the Fish at O'Connell, the Macquarie in Bathurst, there is water pooling in the paddocks, every stream is racing along and the sheep with their twin spring lambs ascamper and the black ubiquitous Angus cattle all shiny and clean from the rain with their calves in the creche. I barely got over the Abercrombie and when I was up by the Tin Shed, there came a text from Deirdre which I pulled off the road to read. You are a great dad, it said. Father's Day, and the Gospel lection for Sixteenth Sunday after Pentecost Luke XIV 25-33, If any man come to me and hate not his father etc. Well suited to the monastery, but Father's Day in a Protestant church?

Ah Christ, Deirdre, you know how to make a man cry, and just as he'd been told he was making some spiritual progress, you took it away.

> A big fan of the rape and the Curse
> I buy them off the plan
> I don't curse and I don't rape
> It would make me less of a man
> The Curse is blue the rape is gold
> Combined they are emerald green
> If you never saw a Purkinje Tree
> You would think them the sweetest sight you had seen

Know where the first Murray Cod was taken by a Gub? Fish River. Surveyor Evans, first white man to see the Bathurst Plains, came down what is still the pick of the valleys.

Make it big

I stayed at the Chifley on South Terrace from which I could see the Adelaide hills over the Parklands from my room on the fourth floor. An hour and a half's walk up Glen Osmond Road to the monastery and a semi-interesting stroll for one who's never before seen Adelaide. I do like quoins in bungalows. The monastery, a white stucco and red terracotta tile affair, stands on the A3 at the intersection with the M1 South Eastern Freeway to Murray Bridge, down which traffic descends in an endless stream towards a set of lights. It was no doubt a secluded spot in 1896, the year the Passionists moved onto a property known as The Glen. That was the year before they took up residence at Ravenswood in Goulburn.

On the corner opposite, a little water feature under a shield of the Kaurna people, proclaiming the Gateway to Adelaide. Behind the water feature, a former convent with padlocked gate as the discalced Carmelite nuns, think Little Flower, moved out in 2010. Part of the wall of the convent beside the A3 has been replaced with bracing ply to mark the spot where a semitrailer hurtling down the M1 failed to take the corner. Opposite the former convent on Glen Osmond Road is a Hungry Jacks and a 24/7 sex shop, 'Adult Bliss'.

Entering the grounds of the monastery, which overlook a soccer pitch, one passes the Passionist Cross featuring the five symbols of the Passion; the dice, the nails, the crown of thorns, the lance, the hyssop stick. There were fifty cars in the carpark and a couple of Ducatis, which puzzled me till I saw the arrowed signs on the grass next to a statue of St Paul of the Cross, Founder of the Congregation, who gestures with his right hand towards the cross he holds in his left, suggesting this is all you will need in the Vale of Tears.

Dollard Room Certificate 3 Work Health and Safety, Foley Room Mission Australia SANDAS.

The Sacred Garden stands at the rear of what would appear to be a conference centre showcasing the fourteen statues that once stood in the garden of Marys Mount. When the Passionists left Goulburn they were moved over the river. When the Mercy convent shut up shop they disappeared for three years.

It was Father Augustine Fitzsimons, novice master at Marys Mount, who conceived the notion of commissioning fourteen marble Stations of the Cross. This likely occurred during a visit to the Rome motherhouse where I had my Passionist interview. Someone there may have known Franco Miozza or had a family connection with the Ferdinando Palla Studio in Pietrasanta. Each statue, which took Miozza eight months to carve, was shipped to Sydney in crate of tongue-and-groove before being trucked over the Razorback. All Stations were present and correct by Good Friday '55, when the Most Reverend Dr Gillie Young assisted by Father Francis Clune CP led a group of Goulburnites on the first perambulation. Among them would have been John Cunningham, a Crooky mate of mine who coughed up fourteen-hundred quid or three years' pay back then to fund a statue for his brother Vince who'd died in a tractor accident. When John heard his statue had disappeared he wrote a letter to the Passionists receiving no reply. Three years later his statue reappeared at the Gateway to Adelaide.

Father John Woods, a Canberra canon lawyer, clarified the matter for John when he told the Goulburn Post in May '03, or a month after the official opening of 'the Sacred Garden' by Premier Mike Rann, 'if they were donated to the Passionists they were free to move them. If they were donated on the condition they would not be moved that would be a different situation. However, a simple understanding on the part of a donor that they 'owned' a statue and it could not be removed would not be sufficient basis for appeal. In the absence of firm evidence to the contrary, the Passionists would assume an acquired right.' Always insist on receipt when dealing with the Black Monks (and watch your arse). There is a plaque by the Sacred Garden containing the names of both John and Vince along with other Goulburn district donors and dedicatees. It is not a prominent plaque. The Garden, we're informed, costs fifty grand a year to maintain (I've just put in my bid for forty-eight) but one-ninety-five bucks buys you a twenty-letter inscription of your choice on a brick of your choice in the brick footpath; six-hundred records your family tree on a brick in the brick wall; eleven-hundred will buy you a memorial plaque on a garden seat while eleven grand will see your name carved on a statue, possibly John's, as well as ensuring a listing for your name on the Garden donor board.

I could never get to Salem myself so was glad to spend the morning strolling round the Purloined Garden. Round and round the Via Dolorosa. I had it to myself though the South Australian Drug and Alcohol workers in the Foley Room could see me just by glancing out a window. By my fourth circuit they're probably wondering, What's he on? I'm now sitting in front of the Fourth Station.

I am also interested in the Ninth Station, Jesus Falls a Third Time. I see Bourke cleaning that Station with his toothbrush. That was the sole occasion I saw the living man. I am interested in the Fourth Station, Jesus Meets his Mother, as that's where Sister Bridge was sitting, according to Sister Edmund, on the morning of Bourke's death when she learned of Bourke's demise. We don't know how she learnt of his demise but she sat in front of that Fourth Station before she borrowed the caretaker's ute and wrote herself off. I don't see that as an accident. The Stations by this stage had moved across the river. As I see her, she has her back toward me and is wearing full kit.

Station Nine, Jesus Falls a Third Time. He looks to be unconscious. He is lying on his right arm. A centurion pulls at his left. He is wearing a stone halo. Simon of Cyrene maintains support of the cross, while behind the cross stands an elder described on the website as 'a symbolic Jewish figure'.

Station Four, Jesus Meets his Mother. Mary dressed as a nun has her right hand on her son's breast and her left on her own. You can see the toes of both, though they could be wearing sandals. Jesus supports the cross with his right hand while his left is on Mary's elbow. His expression is calm. He is wearing his stone halo. He has a moustache and a beard and his long hair falls to his shoulders. His tormentor, gaze fixed on Jesus' head, has clenched a left fist and is raising a vine cane scourge to his right shoulder.

There wouldn't be an RC unacquainted with these Stations though generally as at Christ the King they are paintings or bas relief along a wall. At the Purloined Garden they are white Carrara marble statues, three-foot high, sitting on plinths of aggregate five-foot high by two-foot by four. Thus, you are looking up at the figures as you walk by them but only a bit.

Station One, the Christ is condemned. A calm and contemplative Caucasian convict clad in halo and crown of thorns is cuffed with a rope being held by a sneering Jewish screw who in his free hand shoulders a vine cane scourge. Behind the convict sits the gov, helpless to intervene. He looks half towards us on the path below him half towards the convict. A bowl of water in which he is rinsing his hands is being held by a small boy.

A small-er boy: all these figures in the fourteen Stations are half life-sized but size matters and they would need to be at least life-sized for mine. One thinks of Michelangelo's five-metre-tall David, also of white Carrara marble, that stood in the Piazza della Signoria in Florence from 1503. The year the granite homestead at St Michael's Mercy convent in Goulburn was built is the year the Giant, as the Florentines call him, was moved to the Accademia.

A connection exists beyond Carrara marble: Michelangelo re-established the classical style of sculpture that we see deployed in the Sacred Garden minus Greek paintwork. It is eternally valid being utterly realistic. It is the style of Periclean Athens, the first and artistic ne plus ultra, a point recently emphasized by Alistair Sooke in his three-part series for the Beeb, Treasures of Ancient Greece: TV at its apogee: don't you just hate to see cut-price extras masquerading as historical figures. Books do some things best, but TV for the visual arts.

In further pursuit of the matter, I drove down to Bendigo when I got home to see The Body Beautiful, an exhibition at the Bendigo Gallery showcasing the Townley Diskobolos, a copy of Myron's original with the head fitted the wrong way, taken from Hadrian's villa. Myron, Phidias and Polykleitos were all students of Ageladas the Argive.

A copy of Michelangelo's Pieta adorns the Monastery, but not in the Sacred Garden; adjacent to the A3. It is tucked away amid trees. Michelangelo made his reputation carving that Pieta for St Peters and in the Pieta, as in the Fourth Station of the Cross in the Sacred Garden, the Virgin Mother of God is portrayed as pre-menopausal.

Julius the Second accepted this interpretation of the Virgin. How do we know? Because Julius the Second, seven years after the carving of the Pieta, bad Michelangelo witness the exhumation of the Laocoön on the Esquiline. So Michelangelo was still in his papal benefactor's good books. It was not considered heretical to portray Mary as the same age as Christ.

Michelangelo's Mary is thus not the biological Mother of God and I'm starting to see an object here for Sister Bridge's affections.

> The Sorrowing Mother and her Suffering Son
> In the Fourth Station of the Cross
> Are unveiled by the Florentine psychopompus
> As Ishtar and Tammuz
> The Comforter and her Consort
> The Lord of the Stricken Corn
> Who must die each year at the hand of man
> In order we be reborn

They keep their options open in the Vatican. They are dodgy. You can take a virtual tour of the Sacred Garden at the Monastery website (there could only be one monastery).

> Good old Collingwood forever
> We know how to play the game
> Side by side we stick together
> To uphold the Magpie name
> Hear the barrackers a-shouting
> As all barrackers should
> Oh the premiership's a cakewalk
> For good old Collingwood

Make it new

Before leaving Adelaide I took a tram into town to visit the Art Gallery.

Vouchsafe me an ekphrasis. On the tram I am still thinking of the Stations of the Cross, the wonderful detail, the folds in the cloaks, the fingers, the toes, the anatomical muscular relief, the veins in the arms and the legs, the ribcage in the crucifixion, the facial expressions. The human bodies are less well done than in the Riace bronzes and the folds in the garments less numerous than those in the cloaks of the Parthenon frieze and the figures are diminutive but even so they must have evoked a sense of awe in both Bourke and Sister Bridge. It's as though the two religious were using them as a template. For mine they would need to be slightly larger-than-life-sized, as in the Laocoön, even twice-life-sized like Michelangelo's Tombs of the Medici, or preferably twelve-metres-tall, like the statue of Zeus by Phidias, as a deity should be larger than life and don't let anyone tell you the Virgin Mary is no deity. The Sacred Garden isn't a good place to appreciate a deity. There is noise from traffic and a nearby construction site, the neighbouring houses overlook the garden, there are signs everywhere warning you not to touch the statues, donation boxes, ubiquitous commemorative plaques, hardly the Basilica of San Lorenzo, yet a sense of drama emerges through that sombre, brooding figure, always thoughtful and mysterious, whom I should have thought might have been Joseph of Arimathea but the website identifies as a Cohen.

A sculptor enjoys latitude. No two series of Stations depict the Stations identically. Certain Stations, notably the Seventh, that features Veronica and the Turin Shroud, are unbiblical. In the book I borrowed from Trev, there's a photo of a bas relief of the Fifth Station in which the sculptor has portrayed Padre Pio as St Simon of Cyrene.

When I entered the Art Gallery of South Australia I was confronted in the Melrose Room with a symphony by Philip Glass: an artwork entitled We are all Flesh which consists of two headless horse torsos made of epoxy resin covered in real horse hide hanging from the roof. My consternation was the sought-for response. When I got back to the Chifley and searched the thing on the web, I learned it is the work of the Belgian sculptor Berlinde De Bruyckere and cost the gallery's Collector's Group three-hundred-thousand dollars. Gallery director Nick Mitzevich explains it thus: 'If it is a little bit shocking and disturbing, that's the role of art in the society that we live in now. It is supposed to change our thinking.'

There's an art display by the Gateway
To change the way we think
A selection of ten-inch donkey dongs
In tints of black and pink
We are all flesh say the donkey dongs
Will Venus summon us
As Christ astride his donkey colt
Prepares to mount his Cross?

Need some particulars

When I returned from Adelaide and before my trip to Bendigo I found in the voicemail a reminder I was overdue for an eye test. I wouldn't normally have bothered but having had cataract surgery I thought it best to comply.

It is always interesting to see the new gear they've acquired at the opticians. I was put through the usual battery of tests, being asked is it more or less clear now, and can you read the bottom line, and nothing seemed overly unfamiliar till we came to the dimming of the lights. As the optician, a young Sudanese, a breed I never thought to see in Goulburn, shone a pencil torch into my left pupil I had an extraordinary vision.

'You won't believe this,' I said to him, 'but I just saw some reticulation. It looked like the channel country on a flight from Sydney to Isa.'

'Those are the vessels in your retina,' he said. 'It is called the Purkinje Tree and the wonder is you don't see it all the time because it lies in the light path from the lens. What you just saw we call an entoptic phenomenon. Did it persist?'

'No,' I said in a voice I scarcely recognised. 'Do it again.'

'Let's see if we get it in the right eye. Look to the side for me now that's right. If we keep the torch moving the image may persist.'

So he shines the ophthalmoscope into my right eye and again I see the Purkinje Tree but it doesn't persist.

I can't stop thinking of the Purkinje Tree all the way home. It astounds me I have been looking at my own beautiful capillaries. They formed in my ugly body without my having been aware. I'd seen something beautiful and unexpected and received a boost. God was speaking to me loudly and succinctly.

I am always before your eyes but you never see me. The reason you never see me is because I am always before you. You could not bear my splendour. Mark you I am always there.

I was cooking dinner that night when something welled inside me and I started to cry. What relief. I cried and cried. It was like hearing the opening chords of the second movement of Mahler's Fifth having sat through the senseless and strident first movement. I cried and cried and couldn't stop myself and didn't want to.

I could never have been a Mahler myself; a Poulenc maybe.

We believe in one God
Maker of Heaven and Earth
Of all that is seen and unseen
Beyond the land of birth
And while we have eyes
Before they are covered in dust
We must fill them with tears
To desiccate our calumny
And wash away our fears

Prepare the octopod

It was daughter Fiona informed me Sister Edmund has moved to Young. She got it from her friend Cissy with whom she attends gym.

'You're making bread again, Dad!'

'Yes well there's always something to learn. I find I don't need to add salt to the dough if I let the sweat from my brow drip as I knead.'

'Cissy tells me Sister Edmund has moved to Young. I thought you'd be interested. Olwyn, you be good for Grandpa! Otherwise you won't be able to come out to the farm.'

'I don't want to come out to the farm. I don't like Grandpa. He has horrible ears and smells like a plant that hasn't been watered in years.'

'Don't talk like that. You'll hurt his feelings.'

'No she won't. I don't have any. I did have a shower and put on some aftershave for you, Olwyn. I should perhaps change the aftershave. As to the ears I'm not sure we can do much about those, short of cutting them off. I don't think earrings would help. I wonder has the old girl taken poorly, Fee?'

'Well God Almighty how old would she be now, Dad? Ninety? Ninety-five? Why do they live so long?'

'Punishment. After I've dropped Olwyn back I may call by at their apartments.'

'Oh that bloody car of mine, I just hope the fucking thing starts. Sorry.'

'I wouldn't mind going to Young to see the old girl. I like to see the Canola in flower this time of year.'

'Olwyn! You remember what I said.'

'I want to go home. I'm bored.'

'It's nearly time for Octonauts. Who's your favorite Octonaut, Olwyn? I like Shellington.'

'Kwazii.'

'Here we are then. Just in time. Dah dada dadah da dah da dah dadada dah dada dadah da dah dah dah, then it changes key. Philip Glass never does that. Good God, I'm going to get a drink. Would you like a drink, Olwyn?'

I'd never been off the street at the Mercy apartment block, five single-story units adjoining a side driveway. You wouldn't think it housed religious as the cross on the second unit faces a paling fence. I didn't know which of the five units had been hers so I just went from door to door, no response, yet as I was walking back up the drive a man of late middle years emerges, pretty clearly a priest; fawn slacks, red face, grey comb-over, paunchy. It is indeed a lovely shirt sir, says the Pelaco sign still extant on Murphy's House of Quality in Boorowa. I swear to God the man was wearing a Pelaco shirt.

'Is it about the car? I didn't think it would be in the paper yet.'

'The Nissan Micra.'

'Yes that's her. You can take a look. She's down the back.'

He walked pretty swiftly bad mistake in a vendor.

'Here we are. Low mileage, excellent condition, one elderly driver. Is it for the family member?'

'What you think I wouldn't fit?'

'Ha ha. I'm selling it for another party.'

'You're not a Rabbitohs man. Could I ask a question?'

'Fire away. There's a... logbook... somewhere here... under... just let me... reach...'

'Are you a Passionist?'

I swear he drops the logbook straight onto the seat but quickly recovers, stands up straight as he can and smiles a smile that isn't.

'You can take her for a run.'

'Oh you're too trusting. What if I head for the highway?'

'You won't get far. Here's the key.'

'What price are we thinking?'

'Make an offer.'

He hasn't a clue. It occurs to me if I turn up in Young driving the old vehicle, take her for a spin, it might loosen the haply demented tongue.

'Let's say seven grand. I know this vehicle, I see it about. It's never out of second gear.'

'Cash?'

'You betcha. Here's your deposit. I'll have to fetch the rest.'
'Who shall I make out the rego to?'
'Don't do it yet. Fiona Butterfield but don't do it yet.'
'Very well Fiona. See you shortly, God willing.'

Snug in me Nissan Micra I speed through fields of flowering rape
Dodging old men in lycra cycling towards the victory tape

Would metamorphosis work better for Moses?

How could the Mozia Charioteer ever fall from favour? The human body has improved but the soul has deteriorated. Alistair Sooke insists the Classical style of the Greek Revolution, as exhumed in the *Quattrocento*, appears to have come from nowhere around 500 BC and that itself is plenty weird, for how hard could it be to look at a human body and copy what you saw? The prototypical kouros shows us the germ of the Classical technique and that technique survives yet in the sculpture studios of Pietrasanta, where copies of Greek originals are churned out for today's Asian clientele, assuming they cannot as yet be executed by 3D printer. But the modern European eschews the style of the Sacred Garden as monumental masonry, passé as a bush ballad.

In the main body of the Bendigo Gallery I saw The Shunamite Woman by Giovanni Lombardi from 1865, An Episode of Pompeii by Charles Francis Summers from 1885, Cadorin's Venus Tying her Sandal — in the spirit of the Knidian Afrodite — from 1913 and there's a marble bust of Burns by one John Walter of Bendigo 1911 that you would need to carbon date to ensure it wasn't taken from Hadrian's Villa. To this point taste has not changed. There is a technical falling off but what has happened since? Whatever the damage to the Western soul it is comparatively recent. About the time of the First World War we fell off an aesthetic cliff.

In my mind's eye as I barrel in the Micra through fields of flowering Boorowa Canola, I see one statue speaking to me in the manner of the haka to guide me on my quest. It is the Doryphoros of Polykleitos in the Roman marble copy from Pompeii. I kept returning to it at SBS online until it was no longer there. Sooke calls it the bedrock of Western art, the precursor to Michelangelo's David, the young curly-headed spear-bearer with the comely ears, detached gaze, lifted heel, hip dipped in contrapposto, but most significantly *very* diminuitive penis and calm demeanor. No donkey dong here. The penis is a tiny glans designed for urination. Despite the washboard abs the facial expression is demure.

And no I can't see him as a bottom because he stands six-foot-six. He is a fifth century BC athlete and surely the precursor to our human god of the Trinity though lost a bit of muscle by the time he hangs so wrongly off the Tree. He could pass for Simon called Peter though, a bit on the burly side from hauling nets. He retains his abs in his Buddhist incarnation as the Ghandara Boddhisattva that you could see at the NGA last time I was in Canberra unless it has proved yet another dodgy provenance since returned to the Swat Valley. The Ghandara Bodhisattva is too bulked for mine. He is more saviour than saint, confrontingly masculine, built like Brad Thorn. How William Blake abhorred the muscular crucifixions of Rubens! Rightly so. The muscular man says yes to the world, the Christ and the Buddha say no.

> Men become gods and gods become men
> Traffic either way
> Aristophanes has a laugh
> So your Christ and your Buddha boast arseholes he'd say
> But your student of the Argive counters
> Hits him in the rear of his knees
> Demonstrates the urge to worship
> Is as rational as the urge to sneeze

Rather a bottle in front of me

'Do I know you?'
  'I think you do. My name is Dudley Leahy and we are former colleagues.'
  'I never heard the name.'
  'We worked together in Goulburn Gaol.'
  'I never set foot in a gaol.'
  'Have it your own way. How are you liking Young?'
  'Oh I like'm young.'
  'You're being naughty. I thought we might take a…'
  'What is that bird over there in that paddock, is that a Japanese crane?'
  'No it's an egret. A white cattle egret.'
  'You're very sure of yourself Doug.'
  'I could be mistaken, Sister Edmund, but I think you need to go north if you want to see a Brolga. Try the paddock opposite Gallo's Dairy by the Ganjaburra turnoff.'
  'You and me together, eh? I'm not going. Count me out, Doug.'
  'It's Dud, but you can call me what you like.'
  'As long as I don't call you late for dinner.'
  'Haha. Been a while since I heard that.'
  'As long as I don't call you late for sex. Who do you think has the best *sex*?'
  'Surprise me.'
  'Married women past their prime. What's that crop?'
  'Grapes. That's a vineyard.'
  'Very biblical. Why do we need so many?'
  'Before we could never be drunk enough. Tell me more about women and sex.'
  'I beg your pardon! How *dare* you!'
  'I'm so sorry. Please forgive.'
  'I've a mind to report you.'
  'Don't report me.'
  'To the *police*. I guess you're fond of sex?'
  'I guess. I was once married.'
  'But you wouldn't have sex with a married man?'
  'Good Lord no. Certainly not.'

'So you're not a man who has sex with men but you'd like a bit on the side?'

'Oh give us a break Sister Edmund. We're turning right here toward Harden.'

'Hard-on you say?'

'Oh Christ! You know what's coming up? I'll rephrase that. Did you know what's ahead?'

'Spit it out Doug.'

'A monastery.'

'Turn back.'

I placed my faith in Jesus
Perfection yet afar
But have I turned the stove off
And did I lock my car?
Whenever doubt arises
I wish I had the strength
To banish it from consciousness
As Jesus did at length
Who did his worldly business
Without a worldly fear
As nothing could affright him
On farther shore or near
I never burned the house down
No one stole me wheels
An arid doubt departs me
A deliquescent faith congeals

On yer broom

She has a slight dementia following a slight ischemia which has had the effect of a surreptitious dose of Spanish fly. I was warned she was ingenuous but saw an opportunity.

'This is the Redemptorist Monastery we're driving down the drive toward, Sister.'

We pass the sign reads 'Cead Mile Failte'.

'Clement Mary Hofbauer was a Moravian hermit. There was nothing Irish about Clem.'

'Is that so? I didn't know that. You're a mine of information. I wonder if you could tell me a bit about Marys Mount.'

'Why?'

'Because you know so much.'

'I know you were cut out to be a monk. You've missed your opportunity Doug. They had a juvenate here. A thousand boys came through the place as they couldn't keep up with demand. Mind you that was then and this is now.'

'Too true. Times have changed. The Passionists had their juvenate at St Ives.'

'Here we go. Before you tell me a juvenate is a place where boys are sexually abused, let me ask you this, Dudley Leahy: why would you come all this way except to pick my brain? Don't take me for a fool. Bourke was ordained at age twenty-four in sixty-eight. That's all you'll get.'

'I'll settle for that. Now I'll tell you what I read on the Broken Rites website.'

'Don't bother. I want to get out of the car and go over to the cemetery.'

'Not a problem.'

'I'll need your help.'

'Take my arm. Yes it seems the Passionist paedophile Daniel Lyne was spiritual director at St Ives Juvenate and used the confessional box to seduce young men, many of whom have since come forward.'

'How old were these young men?'

'Fourteen to sixteen years.'

'Old enough to say no.'

'I'll let that pass. In '69 Lyne became rector at Holy Cross College in

Templestowe, the new Passionist Training Centre, because by this time Marys Mount was all but deserted except for Bourke.'

'Has he been charged?'

'Bourke? Oh you mean Lyne. No of course not. His congregation packed him off to Nigeria.'

'It would only have been a hand-job.'

'Is that right? I'm told that Bourke fist-fucked a child and you saw him do it, Sister Edmund.'

'I didn't see him do it.'

You wouldn't put her in a witness box. Could you believe what you just heard?

We drive back to Young in silence though scarcely as silent as Simon Bourke who never spoke in thirteen years except to Sister Bridge: a contumacious felon. As I was turning to drive off, Sister Edmund, so help me God, looked me in the eye and said, 'He never spoke a word. He never said a word in his own defence and I think it may have been a broom-handle.'

It beggars belief that a Christian priest would bugger a boy with a broom
I was born that way I suppose he might say if another came into the room
It was done to me so I pass it along
It's a rite of passage at old St John
A seminal seminarian song
A bit of harmless fun

High sider

They'd a bike swop at the Showground Sunday so I went along hoping to find a few parts for Twomey's KTM which he came off bigtime, silly old prick. He was in all sorts; did his tib and fib. I was wandering round when I spy Hec Cartwright recently retired plumber though won't answer to the word 'retired' and I'm a bit the same. Luckily, no such thing as a retired cattleman. Hector was exhibiting his WLA Harley. He can still kick start it. Always attracts admirers and a bit of conversation. Being an orphan from the orphanage who attended St Michael's Ag and Trade, Hec is the one man I know who lived with Bourke at the orphanage. In contrast, half Goulburn went through school with Simon Bourke and all Goulburn knows what happened to him in the Gaol, how he came to grief. You can blame me for that. From what I gather, Bourke came across as a normal Catholic boy. That's a normal Catholic adolescent, pre-pill, pre-abortion on demand.

'How's it goin' there, Hec.'
'Oh hello Dudley. Nice day.'
'Yes beautiful. Mate, I'll wait till you've a moment as there's something I'd like to ask.'
'It's about Bourke. Christ, you're that persistent you remind me of my old blue heeler, who the minute you sit at the barbecue drops that filthy old tennis ball at your feet and stands staring at it till you pick it up awash in his slime and slobber and throw it for him, because if you merely kick it he'll always block it. You're still on the case.'
'Won't take a moment. It's about the culture at the orphanage.'
'We didn't have one. Next question.'
'I'm using the word loosely. Was there any bastardization of younger boys by older ones?'
'No. You've drawn another blank, Dud.'
'Thanks anyway.'
'I won't have anyone criticising the Mercy Sisters. They did a good job. Old Sister Maddy was a treasure and I still recall Sister Edmund very young and pretty.'
'Christ, how old are you?'

'Old as me tongue and a little bit older than me teeth.'

'Regarding Sister Edmund, would you recall when she left the orphanage to teach in Boorowa?'

'No. I know she was working in the gaol when the orphanage closed.'

'Is that right? I didn't know that. Are you sure?'

'I am. There was a function held at the Worker's Club to which I got an invite. The MC made a big joke of her working in the gaol. I recall that because I still had a thing for her.'

> I sit within the anchorhold
> To fix my mind on God
> A God who likes me virginal
> I find that passing odd
> For if he didn't fashion me
> Who exactly did?
> And if he's made a blunder
> Of God I would be rid

Goostli werk

Would you believe she's passed? Wouldn't it rot your socks. I just drove back to Mt St Joseph's to ask her a few questions and found she's gone. I wanted to see if she'd give the same answer to questions I already posed plus I had a few fresh ones and she's gone. She was only ninety-two.

She may well have been Catholic chaplain in '73. The first three government-funded chaplains were appointed to Long Bay in '62 but that said, the notion of prison as penitentiary was central to Port Arthur. A penitentiary addresses itself to the soul, a prison to the body. We no longer have souls, so a chaplain today has to prove worth in bodily rather than ghostly terms; time spent by clients in segro and the like. The Nagle Royal Commission of '78 on the riots of the early '70's found chaplains had dogged on inmates, so now they answer only to the Church though they're not allowed to proselytize. When I quit Goulburn, we'd Sister Edmund full-time government funded, the Rev Trev full-time government funded, a Sally two days a week paid but not government funded, a Buddhist one day a week unpaid and a Muslim one day a week but full-time elsewhere and government funded. The chapel complex in G-block has an interview room and an office, but owing to the ukase of two chaplains at all times, an imam doesn't use it. It's all prayer mats in Prislam, aka SuperMax and the Leb yard.

Why appoint a trained teacher like Sister Edmund to the chaplaincy? If Bourke was in fact guiltless and yard gossip bullshit, who better placed than Sister Edmund to initiate the gossip?

I have worked it out. In '73, ex hypothesi, Sister Edmund could have sat on gaol committees. So I wanted to ask if ever she sat on a three-person committee comprising herself, Governor Mumbles and AS Laid-Back Lester: the Catholic Mafia of Goulburn Penitentiary.

I just wanted a reaction.

If I saw what I saw then I can't anymore
Believe that he did what they say
He would never have done what that tiresome old nun
Has alleged but it won't go away
From break of dawn till I drain my last dram
I hear his ghostly tread
It's as though he believes he is still alive
And I am the man who is dead

Lif contemplatif

And the chief priests accused him of many things: but he answered nothing. And Pilate asked him again saying Answerest thou nothing? Behold how many things they witness against thee. But Jesus yet answered nothing; so that Pilate marvelled

Mark XV 3-5

Attention George Pell: A man who is truly humble is not indignant when he is wrongly accused and says nothing to justify himself against false accusation but accepts slander as truth. He does not attempt to persuade people he is calumniated but begs forgiveness. Some have voluntarily attracted accusations they did not merit and have wept asking their offenders forgiveness for the iniquity they had not done their soul all the while being utterly pure and chaste. A man who can bear an injury with gladness even if he holds in his hands the means to repel it receives comfort from God for his faith. And a man who humbly suffers accusations made against him has reached perfection and the holy angels marvel at him. For no other virtue will be as high or as hard to practise

St Isaac of Nineveh

The more difficulties in life the more I hope in God. I hope that God will save me through the merits of the Passion of Jesus. I rejoice in the nails that hold me crucified

St Paul of the Cross

Hold your tongue when suffering a wrong!

St Columbanus

There were occasions an inmate would materialize within a wing who didn't fit the mould. He would only be there a few months. As AS, you would suspect an Intel operative working undercover but it would never be confirmed. Once, on secondment as PO One at LBH, I was given a nod and a wink when I couldn't locate a particular file, so it does happen. Men do time outside of remand who have never faced a court and never will, and knowing the system as I do, and given Goulburn was Tyke Central, I conclude the turning of a few blind eyes at the appropriate juncture has served here to facilitate what we might call a ghostly experiment. And it was done effectively, all paperwork shredded, if it ever existed. And the Passionists were not sending us a message in not defrocking Bourke; they couldn't be bothered. There's a frocked priest in the US currently doing time for murder, while convicted religious rockies are rarely if ever expelled. Their congregation usually gives them a house and a car when they get out of boob.

What a pity the boys in Rome decided it was all for naught and wouldn't take the word of a certain green baggy.

As to whether an infant boy was assaulted in the Orphanage, the Catholic instinct in such a case is to move the victim interstate and the perpetrator too, but if the perpetrator here were an older orphan, surprised in flagrante delicto, and the wounds were serious, then Bourke on the spur of the moment may well have chosen to bite his tongue. He may have felt he had no choice. He may have had no choice. He was certainly about the place.

There would have been those who understood. They would have included Mumbles and Laid-Back Lester and I go further: had Bourke become a *son* then he would have been bearing the sins of the world. He would have realised the monastery was moribund. He knew the gaol was doing nicely. A quick trip down the hill and over the river, he's in a better place.

The activity of cross-bearing is of two kinds; one consists in enduring bodily afflictions; the other consists in contemplation. Every man who before perfecting his training in the first passes to the second being attracted by its delights not to speak of his own laziness becomes overtaken by wrath for not having first mortified his 'members which are upon the earth' (Col. III 5) that is, for not having overcome the impotence of thoughts by patient exercise in the activity of bearing the cross and for presuming to let his mind dream of the cross' glory. This is the meaning of the saying of the saints of old that if a man's mind conceives an intention to climb on to the cross before his senses are cured of their sickness and have achieved a state of serenity, he is overtaken by the wrath of God. A man whose mind is defiled by shameful passions, who is quick to fill it with fantasies, has an interdiction set upon his lips, because without first purifying his mind by suffering,

without conquering carnal lusts, he puts his trust on what his ear has heard and what is
written in ink and has forged ahead on a path shrouded in darkness

St Isaac of Nineveh

Was he guilty of deception if he never entered a plea?
Could a man be born of a virgin so unscientifically?
In a world of total silence
Query is absurd
Time dissolves in teardrops
Logic is deferred

Man on the ground

To bring me back to earth I just had a call from eldest daughter Shirl. I did the math: she must be pushing fifty, haven't heard from Shirl in some time. Senior public servant lives on the slopes of the Black Mountain, no children, probably cosseting a Labradoodle. Used to be married, never liked him. Sort of man who wouldn't look when a motorbike went by.

'Don't tell me he picked the bloody thing up! That you, Dad?'

Shirl sounds a bit like Deirdre on the phone, so I hesitated, which I shouldn't have done. Gave her the wrong impression.

'We don't need to talk if you'd rather not, in fact you can go and get fucked.'

'Please don't say that. I'm only trying to work out who you are.'

'Don't bother. I've the wrong number.'

'Is that you, Deirdre?'

'It's actually Shirley, your eldest daughter Shirley. Remember me?'

'Don't be like that, Shirl. You do sound like Deirdre on the phone.'

'You're a little deaf. Now the next thing you always ask is how may I be of assistance, so let me spell it out and you won't need to. I'd like you to come to lunch Sunday. Do you know the address?'

'Of course I know the address. Will there be others there?'

'What if I say no.'

'That's fine by me.'

'What if I say yes.'

'I don't mix terribly well Shirl.'

'You don't mix at all. I'll see you round one. I suppose you'll go to church?'

'Oh, you know what a hypocrite I am there, Shirley.'

'Come after church.'

'What should I bring?'

'Just bring your ears, Big-Ears.'

'Ha. That takes me back.'

'It's been a while since we spoke, Dad.'

'Yes, too long.'

'You could have rung.'
'I could have. I don't know what to say.'

She doesn't like me which is why I never ring. Sunday when I got outside the house and saw the three cars including the Nissan Micra, I realized I'd been ambushed.

'I think the last occasion I saw my girls all together was at their mother's funeral. What's the occasion today?'

'Your birthday.'

'Is that a fact? Come to think of it I did change my smoke alarm battery this morning.'

'We're concerned about you, Dad.'

'Concerned?'

'We'd like to discuss a few things.'

'I'm not sure I understand. But then I should have guessed, because a birthday at my age is no cause for celebration, not that I don't appreciate the trouble you've gone to Shirl, getting us all together and that. Is there someone minding Olwyn, Fee?

'No I leave her alone with a chainsaw, Dad.'

'What's for lunch?'

'Thought we might go out.'

'Excellent! Great idea. Come on Orla, give us a spin in your Pug!'

Orla designs climbing walls. She lives in Newtown with another woman in what they construe as a marriage and Brenda encouraged her.

'First we need to discuss a few things with you, Dad.'

'Oh, it's a set-up. I should have guessed.'

'Why must you be so hostile?'

'I'm not being hostile.'

'We should go to lunch, Deirdre. Dad's probably tired.'

'Alco's are always tired.'

'I think we need to say to him what needs to be said before lunch.'

'I think I'll go home. I don't want to have this conversation.'

'Dad!'

'I'll go for a stroll.'

'You might get lost.'

'For Chrissake, let him have his lunch in peace!'

'Don't take the Lord's name in vain if you don't mind. I've just come from church and I'd like no comment on that.'

'He'll want a drink and then he'll fall asleep on the couch.'

'Who do you people think I am? You speak as though I weren't here.'

'That's good. Your own daughters are you people.'

'Why do you go to church, Dad? I can be in touch with God without going to church. I need only look at all the beauty in the world'.

'That is the heresy of the Free Spirit, Deirdre, that arose following the Papal Schism. We all need to go to church.'

'Tell us why you go to church, go on. It hasn't improved you.'

'I don't think anyone needs to explain why they go to church. To improve themselves.'

'It hasn't improved you.'

'Yes, so you say. Well I'm not yet pure in heart but I am working on it. No need to repeat yourself.'

'I learned that from you.'

'Oh Christ, why did we think this was a good idea?'

'It was your suggestion!'

'Let's start again. Happy birthday, Dad!'

'Thanks heaps, Orla! Thanks to yez all for making the effort. I do love yez all. I hope you know that.'

'We love you too but how long can you expect to stay on Willochra? Do you hold a current driver's license?'

'Fuck me dead what's this about? You trying to book me into a home?'

'You *are* an old man. When did you last see a doctor?'

'What business is that of yours?'

'Every business. Fee tells us you have cancer.'

'Oh, it's only prostate cancer. All men my age have it.'

'I had a call the other day from Deakin Oncology, Dad. They want to know why you never came in for your post-operative check-up.'

'Because it's not compulsory.'

'You pig-headed old prick. As if it weren't bad enough losing Mum to cancer. A nice job you did on her as well.'

'Thanks Shirl.'

'It wasn't just the one phone call. I've had several. Why do you never answer your phone?'

'Because no one likes the cold call from Hyderabad. You won't get me to a doctor, Deirdre, and no law says I have to go. I do have a few aches and pains but that's normal at my age.'

'Fee says she often finds you bent over in agony.'

'That's only when I'm watching the evening news.'

'What are you out to prove here, Dad?'

'Nothing.'

'You mobile is always switched off. You don't respond to a text. You don't have an email address. You're not on Facebook. You never visit anyone. You never pick up your mail. You couldn't be bothered attending your own grandson's graduation!'

'Oh I'm sorry. I didn't know it was on. How did he go?'

'First class honours. Julian was actually quite disappointed you weren't there.'

'I'll bet. But I will apologize when next I see him. Convey my congratulations. What now girls? Break out the champers? I haven't been much of a father to you, or a grandfather to your children, I do accept that. What can I say except that I've had other things on my mind? I know it's no excuse.'

'More important things. You've been a good father to Fiona. We didn't all miss out.'

'Oh let's not go there please. He did his best.'

'It wasn't up to much. Yes you're quite right, Orla, I was a dud Dad. Dud Leahy. Dud most things actually but am fully engaged at present in trying to solve an important mystery.'

'Best price on single malts? I think we've heard enough. I think we might forget lunch, girls. Let's all pig out at the All You Can Eat Bistro at the Burns Club.'

'You're losing your marbles, Daddy. You've PTS from that bloody gaol. You never should have taken the job. What on earth made you do it?'

'Literature. We boast more than Miles Franklin in Goulburn. We boast

Jimmy Dwyer. In 1900 a spell in our dark cells produced Jimmy's immortal 'The Lost Button'. Not read Jimmy? He was bigger than Colleen McCullough. No seriously, penury. Inherited debt. Desire to see you fed and clad. I'm actually glad I took the job as it's given me a Weltanshauung.'

'You're a crashing bore and an alcoholic and all thanks to the job.'

'Leave it Orla.'

'No. He's lost it. We have a responsibility to him. He lives like a pig in a pigsty.'

'Is that what you tell them, Fiona?'

'Well no, not exactly.'

'Fuck the lot of yers! I'm out of here. How sharper than a serpent's tooth, you pack of shrews you want me in a home! Anything to get your paws on the rent from the wind farm.'

'That would barely cover your costs. As to Willochra, the gates are a disgrace...'

'They are my workout. Cheaper than a gym.'

'... there's grass growing out of the gatepost, the fences are falling apart, the paddocks are full of junk and weeds, the house is a knockdown. We think you should take a medical. That's all we're asking here. Not much to ask. It's for your own benefit. You owe it to yourself.'

'I'll do it within the year.'

'Is that a promise? Look me in the eye. I'm holding you to that. Look me in the eye now! Say it again!'

'No! Stop giving me orders.'

'He's doing the best he can, Shirl, but he's losing weight. Look at the man. Skin and bone.'

'He's an alcoholic. You saw him in action at Mum's wake. He drank a whole bottle of whisky. That's twenty-four standard drinks. Then he drove home! Look at the rings around his eyes. Look at the veins in his nose.'

'Oh this is getting nasty. I don't know why yez invited me. Has anyone here ever seen me drunk?'

'We told you. We want you to see a doctor. It's a wonder you're not dead. It's only because we love you, Dad.'

'I'll do it in my own good time.'

152

'We could insist you know. Don't push it, mate. Next of kin.'

'Ho ho ho in the ACT perhaps, but I live in New South Wales! You have no power of attorney. Did I give you power of attorney?'

'Let's leave it, please. Let's not spoil the occasion.'

'The occasion is spoiled.'

'We've organised you a present, Dad.'

'Stick it. Take me to the Burns Club, I'll eat myself to death.'

That's the way it's always been when women mass. Not good though, is it? Why do daughters always think they know what's best for others? Star Bistro at the Burns Club in Kambah is worth a look. Be warned: there's always a queue at the door. All you can eat in the Bistro. Best to book ahead.

You didn't realise how much you could eat now did you?

And the present? Well it came as a pleasant surprise though no doubt intended as a joke as it cost them nothing. They booked me into the guesthouse at Tarrawarra Abbey. Visiting Munster, I'd meant to stay at Mt Melleray or Mt St Joseph Roscrea but they were both booked out, it being mid-summer. Lots of cheapskates bludge their way round Europe staying in abbeys. There's actually a website Good Night and God Bless. Chapter 53 of the Benedictine Rule states a guest must be welcomed as though he were the Christ ('I was a stranger and ye took me in' Matthew XXV 35). No charge is levied for full board and lodging though it would be poor form not to make a small donation.

Bain marie upon bain marie of haggis and gristled snoot
With tatties and neeps for afters
Was what wee Rabbie was all aboot
But that's history in Kambah
Fancy a chow mien
Accompanied by basil pasta
And some maple syrup on your lamb loin
With a bowl of coconut curry
Dusted with fresh parmesan cheese
And a Mexican jalapeno
On some vannamei prawn from the Thai seas

A young Asian girl will clear your plate
The minute you pause your fork
Then it's off for the big gelato
But you're side-tracked by that candied pork

No champers at my birthday party but the Abbey of Clairvaux in Champagne was visited by the first Irish Cistercian Gillacrist O'Conarchy and Gillacrist founded Mellifont Abbey near Drogheda in 1157. That'll do me. Clairvaux — since the days of the French Revolution a high-security prison, nowadays France's SuperMax incarcerating, among other notable scumbags, Carlos the Jackal — was a daughter house of Citeaux, as was the Abbey of Loroux and Pontron was a daughter house of Loroux, and Pontron begat Melleray and the monks of Melleray Abbey founded Mt Melleray Abbey in Waterford following the French Revolution and eight-hundred acres of Goulburn land, a tidy parcel, was bequeathed by a cousin of mine to Mt Melleray Abbey a century on, and Mt Melleray Abbey begat the Southern Star Abbey of Kapua NZ where Baxter took retreat, and also Mt St Joseph Roscrea Tipperary, and Tarrawarra in the Yarra Valley is a daughter house of Roscrea.

There were eventually in Ireland forty-two Cistercian filiations of Mellifont Abbey. Austerity comported with Celtic tradition, while the Trappist Reformists were the analogues of Ireland's eighth-century Celi De-Culdee. But following dissolution by Thomas Cromwell and later if modest re-establishment, since the nineteen-sixties it has become a struggle for any abbey to maintain a quorum of twelve religious.

It was Deirdre's idea. She's been watching Public Enemy Series One on SBS, a Belgian drama in which a putrid rocky is improbably released into the care of the novice master at Vielsart Trappist Abbey in the Ardennes. I couldn't watch it. It exploits the reputation of Belgium as the home of both fine Trappist beers and paedophiliac SVPs.

Isaac of Stella, English-born abbot of twelfth century Aquitaine, describes the monastery as a 'hell of mercy' with the abbot as 'father of souls and torturer of bodies'. I think Mumbles would have approved that.

Pax

Being the sole inscription at the abbey entrance on the Healesville-Yarra Glen Road. Peace in Latin. A somewhat defiant gesture post-Vatican Two as the only Latin you'll hear during retreat at Tarrawarra is Salve Regina, which is sung in the dark as the final hymn of Compline. With more spirit than the psalms preceding, always four and ninety-one, but the singing, all in Gregorian unison, is frankly bloody dreadful. The congregation turns toward the rear of the chapel to Notre Dame, depicted as a thirty-something brunette with a quizzical expression wearing a blue veil and holding open in her right hand a codex, presumably her psalter. I dare say the Virgin could read Latin, though in the stained-glass window of St Anne at St Patrick's Church, Boorowa, Anne's little Venetian-blonde daughter with the halo is being taught square Hebrew. As artwork, the portrait in Tarrawarra is no Lippo Lippi but it does the job in the dark.

The rest of the chapel is worthy of Grand Designs. It needs to be. Chapel is crucial in the life of the monk who is in and out of chapel day and night. The guesthouse, within earshot of the button-operated bell, which was right outside my bed, in fact I'd say about a metre away, is the former bolthole of David Syme, publisher of The Age, and not without its own wainscoted charm. The ceilings are white-painted boards. It could be described as heritage in that the floorboards creak and there are no en suites.

Floorboards in the chapel are brilliantly polished honey-coloured tongue-and-groove and don't creak as yet. They are immaculate. You can see the Led light reflections from the ceiling as you bow your head and hang your arms in the lesser doxology said after each psalm: Glory be to the Father and to the Son and to the Holy Spirit as it was in the beginning, is now and ever shall be, world without end. Is the world without end? Cosmologists claim that nothing lasts forever but what would cosmologists know. I couldn't dignify the singing in chapel with the word 'chant' but enjoyed the striking visual impact of the monks in their black-and-white clobber. Modern and efficacious both, the sanctuary has large blocks of wood, also honey-coloured, that serve as altar and lectern, before a tapestry of the Cross with the transom off-centred: a brilliant touch that.

And appropriate, because the choir stalls down each side of chapel number forty in all, but never saw I more than ten monks in the white cowl and habit, black scapular, brown leather cincture, any old socks and shoes; Adidas trainers, Ugg boots. There are fourteen professed monks but one is infirmarian, another in his care. No novices, no postulants, eighteen in the cemetery. A further seven monks in NZ, five short of a quorum, makes a total of twenty-odd Trappist monks in all Oceania.

I went as Christ in disguise on a cold wet week in the Yarra Valley, mid-June. Several elderly founders from Roscrea still attend chapel. They ventured from Europe the year before Goulburn's fourteen Stations of the Cross and because they never leave the abbey they retain the Irish accent. It is infectious. Whenever an old boy gave a reading the rest of us became a tad Irish as we recited our psalms antiphonally, one side of chapel bellowing at t'other.

The 'three fifties', as the Dark Age Irish called the psalter, are bad enough in Latin. In English they are dire. In Hebrew they must have had something going for them, what it is now hard to see. Rhythm? They are so repetitious and so banal, except when rivers clap hands and the like, yet they constitute the main body of worship in that horrid English doggerel. In the Cistercian golden age they were thought to be the work of King David. Well there never was a King David and anyway, David just means King so that David David is David David.

My heart warmed to the Irish founders. There were three of them. Father Finbarr played the organ not very well. A competent organist would be most welcome as a novice. You didn't need to go to Eire at all, Dad, as Deirdre remarked: indeed Deirdre, and it would have been better to have gone in the seventh century when Clonard, Clonfort, Bangor, Clonmacnoise, Glendalough and their ilk held hundreds if not thousands of monks. That would have generated a different vibe. Amid the oaks of Ireland's Bangor seven choirs of three-hundred boys sang hymns in shifts night and day. There were seven-hundred-odd monks at St Bernard's SuperMax Convent in Clairvaux . A different vibe. Eire in the Dark Ages was the most civilized nation in Europe, according to Thomas Merton, a few books by whom were in the bookshelf at the top of the guesthouse stairs. I had to read them as no TV. Monks are allowed to watch TV in their post-Black Saturday fireproof bunker but only Sunday night.

Vale Regina it's Midsomer Murders. We need to see the beginning.

Mid-afternoon. You approach the abbey via a sinuous, well-maintained dirt drive. I was driving the ute, grille still adorned with three-month-old baked-on yellow grasshoppers, when I happened on a man of Melanesian appearance in a Kubota tractor with a square bail of oaten hay on the forks. I instinctively stopped. He was heading for a gate beyond which stood a mob of bellowing Angus.

'Open the gate for ya, mate?'

'Ta.'

'These boys yours?'

'Yeah. Getting out of the Charolaise into the red Angus.'

'Oo. I'd be headin' for Murray Grey. Truth to tell they're a tad Charolaise. Not a fan of these red Angus.'

Having considered my remark he turns off the tractor engine. Then, as the bellowing intensifies, he jumps down from the cab. I get out of the ute. Slouched over the bonnet we engage in a duologue on the relative merits of various beef breeds and the current price per kilo fetching in Goulburn that goes on half an hour. Eventually I'm like, I have to be going, I'm booked into the guesthouse. Oh, he says, I might see you round. Didn't think he was a monk. Wasn't wearing the clobber. One time they always wore the clobber even when mucking out the pig-pen. Even when milking the cows. I could see the ruins of the milking shed. Every convent should have one.

Every convent does have one.

The guest master squeezes into a cubicle in one of a warren of wooden rooms off a small hall. Opposite is the guesthouse kitchen in which you wash your dishes and make your breakfast. The monks eat in their own refectory. They reputedly lunch in silence while listening to a suitable reading in the main meal of the monastic day but talk during dinner in the evening after Vespers.

As I was turning to climb the stairs that led me to my room, I said to Brother Bob who was wearing the black-and-white clobber 'Who's that bloke manages your cattle? We just had a bit of a chat.'

'Big man? Melanesian ? Would have been Dom Carthage. He likes driving that tractor.'

I'd got off on the right foot with the Abbot.

Very quiet in the guesthouse at night. Just the possum coming and going in the roof cavity, an occasional beep from the answering machine on the phone in the guest master's cubicle. I couldn't say it woke me. I was never in more pain. Isaac of Stella would have approved. I was glad when three a.m. came round and it was time to get up.

Pain! What is it? No man can say. Maybe it's good for us, pain. It's like the soul in that we cannot assay another's pain. No man can prove a plaintiff's back don't hurt: ask the compo lawyer.

> Sons of a hard-on, sons of unchaste mothers
> We deserve better than this
> And so tender and compassionate Virgin
> Who gives eternal birth to your eternally suffering Son
> Restrain we beseech you the elbow of the Mighty
> As He raises above us His dreadful sword of Justice
> And whisper in His terrible ear
> 'These before you were only men with arseholes
> Innoculated in parturition with their own mother's shit
> What more could you have expected, Son?'
> Pure undefiled immaculate Virgin
> Mother aunty sister and fiancee
> Bestow on us a glance from your merciful eyes
> Even as the goodman longs for a stiff whisky at the end of a hard day's
>   work in the cattleyard *Selah*
> Even as the goodman longs for an ice-cold ale
>   brimming in a broad schooner glass *Selah*
> We long for your affectionate glance
> When the temperature soars at noontide and the wheat is ripening
> Our enemies laugh at us and say to one another
> 'Look at them. Where is their Virgin Mary now?
> Forsooth they are fit only for the nursing home'

We plead for your unconditional love
We endure our exile
In this vile vale of lamentations
In which everything we have tried to do we have failed in
To pray that you dry our tears in the abundant hair of your head
To ask of you that you enfold us in your comfortable bosom
In hope that you will say to us at the end of this life
Go to sleep
I shall protect you from His judgement
Go to sleep
Go to sleep now my beloved and rest in peace

We had a sign over the gate at Goulburn Gaol too but only on the inside of the gate.

You'll be back you piece of shit.

Watching

Four a.m. I haven't eaten the night before not wanting to meet fellow guests. Not wanting further palaver. Am on an alcohol fast.

Ten monks turn out in the cold and rain all wearing full clobber. I sit in the side chapel. As you'd expect there was coughing and rumbling of stomachs and clearing of throats but Vigil is a major hour with no musical accompaniment. A heavy emphasis on the cursing of enemies in the prescribed psalms. Dom Carthage from his choir stall made no indication he recognised me and I was the only non-monk there. Winter Vigil is a big ask.

I had the visuals as they should have been, albeit I was prepared. I'd seen, at the Cremorne Orpheum, *Into Deep Silence*, filmed in the Grand Chartreuse in 2005, a study of the austere life in a Carthusian charterhouse. I'd seen, at the Paddington Chauvel, *Of Gods and Men* by Xavier Beauvois, 2010, a dramatization of the murder during the Algerian War of Independence of seven French Trappist monks at Tibhirine Abbey in the Atlas, so I knew what to expect, but everything is a trifle unreal at four on a winter's morning and it felt weird to be watching in real time these strange men from the past in their antique garb with their abstruse misogyny. Just me to see it, though anyone can see it. I'm only up and about at four on a winter morning if I'm taking a piss or can hear a fox upsetting the chooks in the chook house. In the latter case I'm debating whether to lose time and get dressed or race out in the nude. Usually ends up a bit of both. I keep the Kalashnikov by the door.

Vigil concluded at four-thirty when the bellringer monk pressed the button that rings the bell in the belltower. He rang the bell in two blocks of three followed by one of nine. Eighteen bells in all: the Irish Angelus. The one you hear at six p.m. on Or Tee Ee TV. The one you hear in Machattie Park in Bathurst at nine a.m. Saturday. The peal rings out over the abbey's three-hundred acres of prime vineyard land with no vineyard down to the Yarra River. Beyond the river you can see the headlights of early morning traffic heading toward Melbourne.

Back to bed if not to sleep but up again in the dark for Mass-and-Lauds at six. I dare say the Irish founders would have it all pretty fine-tuned. In their late eighties, early nineties, they'd probably need only five minutes to wake up, take a piss, get dressed and stumble to chapel. They're probably still half asleep all through the service. They're probably sound asleep in bed again ten minutes after the final bell. It would structure their dreams.

A few cars were driving up as I walked the short distance from the guesthouse. I could see the headlights in the distance, winding round the drive. They harbour locals who make a point of attending Mass each day; a drop-out Jesuit priest with his young Asian wife, and a few odds and sods. The locals occupied vacant stalls, ruining the visual. Two of my three fellow guests were seated with me in the side chapel though one pointedly failed to attend a single service the whole time I was there.

A young Malaysian Chinese with Hokkien accent was celebrant: he'd be your man playing with his laptop on the website, monk of the future.

How could I fudge it through a Catholic Mass? All too easy, mate: actually, shock horror, not so different from the Anglican. They even gave me the blood. Indeed, if you want a full cantillation with full bells and smells, attend a Solemn High Mass at Christ Church St Laurence. There you will get the full poofter Anglo-Catholic experience. There you will hear a missa brevis from one of Sydney's best choirs.

I used occasionally to attend the oldest church in Sydney, Francis Greenway's fully refurbished Georgian St James at the corner of Phillip and King, but one time when the clerk kept rabbiting on about his 'partner' in the sermon, I thought what's that about? If she's not your wife, who is she? I now attend Christ Church St Laurence by Central Station. As a man who can't stand a clerk dressed as a stockbroker, I steer well clear of St Andrew's though it's another Blacket cathedral.

I didn't sleep between Vigil and Mass. That is the time for lectio divina, reading as tasting and eating, meditation as chewing. No bells after Mass. I kept thinking of Brenda. Shirley was right there when she implied I could have done better. Unfinished business. I should have done better. I should have been more understanding. Pardon's the word. But mostly I think of Simon Bourke at the Presentation Retreat. I'm in his element.

Do I pray to God? No. I pray to the Blessed Virgin. I get on board. Vigil replaces Matins in the rescheduling of the Benedictine hours. I was never one for prayer supplicatory, give me this and give me that, but I felt in view of my setting

— the splendid parsimony of my shabby single bed, reading chair, bar radiator, the desk and on the wall the crucifix, a copy of the Lord's Prayer, the chubby Renaissance-style Virgin and Child — a bedroom not unlike that of Padre Pio, who lived in pain, I should make an exception.

So I make an exception.

Give me understanding and I shall live! I want to know what happened and why, that night back there in A-wing.

Knock and it shall be opened unto you
In Matthew's metaphor of the door
And a door has handles one to either side
So who it is that opens up we can't be sure
Seek and ye shall find suggests we open it ourselves
In a manifestation so to speak
Though some would visualize an unseen hand
Nudging from its hiding place some item that they seek
If whosoever asketh receiveth
Then I have asked with insufficient vim
If we think of prayer as an isthmus
Where His journey towards us confronts our journey towards Him
But if it's Christ doing the asking here
And his Mother who is knocking at the door
And his Father who is looking for some answers
I mustn't keep them waiting anymore

Waiting

What occupation can a monk have in his cell except to mourn? His very seclusion and solitude by their likeness to life in a tomb far from human joys teach a monk that his work is to mourn. All the saints have left this life in mourning

St Isaac of Nineveh

There is no holiness in sadness

Papa Frank (Pope Francis)

Three-hundred odd Christian Brothers survive in Australia though many now retired. No recruits over the past ten years. Average age seventy-five. Most cajoled into the congregation as junior brothers aged fourteen. As their provincial leader recently told the Royal Commission 'this stunted their psychosexual development and they were uneasy with adult relationships. Their dominance over young people exerted itself in a very catastrophic way.' The congregation is wealthy through the sale of orphanage land though forty-eight million dollars has gone out to compensate victims of sexual abuse. As recently revealed by the Royal Commission through data taken from the Church's own files, fully one in five Australian Christian Brothers are alleged paedophiles. Add to these the more than one in ten diocesan priests, the one in five Marist Brothers, the one in five Salesians of Don Bosco and a little fewer than half the Brothers of St John of God and we have in this country a formidable congregation of religious perverts. In fact, we take the international gold medal for Catholic kiddie-fiddling. Nowhere else has the Church recorded such abominable appetency. It's as well they're rarely charged; we'd have to pack them in as they do the felons in the Philippines. They'd be asleep in the stairwells. We'd be tripping over them.

When the early Church borrowed the festival of Easter from the cult of Cybele, it neglected to filch the attendant rite of hieratic castration, preferring to enjoin chastity, an adjuration repealed by Luther, Austin Friar who fucked a Cistercian nun. Were the dog-collared pervert a eunuch, his propensity for sexual abuse of minors would be curtailed, and I know men who'd do the job. There would be no charge. Just a thought.

Christ is a jealous lover and so too His mother.

When those who've pledged the faith recant
One act remains we cannot scant
Yes that remains which liberates
The spirit from the flesh
An act of sacrifice through which
All living trees their roots refresh
An act that frees the saintly man
From every taint that wise men scorn
The contract with the warrior
In payment for the booze and porn

Together with a moustachioed woman who doesn't have much to say and a brash Koori from Swan Hill, an old pot-bellied Christian Brother shares our guesthouse table. It is he advises his dinner plate that half these Trappists are on the pension. No vineyard despite three-hundred acres of prime vineyard land. The brother speaks to his dinner plate pausing only to masticate and always helps himself to seconds and thirds. He'd have enjoyed the Burns Club.

To preclude excursions, we're expected to eat a hot luncheon in the guesthouse. When I sought to remain in my room one day someone came to fetch me.

The food? Pretty ordinary. Boarding-house fare but plenty of it.

There are three short services held daily at the minor hours. In between Terce and Sext the monks do a little physical work. A versicle, a brief reading, a couple of psalms, ten minutes or so, look it up on Wikipedia Liturgy of the Hours, I won't bore you with it. I have been notified I am a crashing bore. Having earned some cred through having attended Vigil at four a.m., I stood in the choir stalls at Terce and found the acoustic much improved. No organ accompaniment. No tintinnabulation. Terce at eight, my third service for the day and the sun had barely risen.

Sext at eleven fifteen a.m. ten minutes. Check it out on Wikipedia post-Vatican Two Revised Liturgy. A versicle, a hymn, a brief reading from the breviary, a couple of psalms but the bell was rung again in three blocks of three followed by one of nine. The Irish Angelus. I stood at the Notre Dame end of chapel and when the monks turned towards the Cross I couldn't see anything of my own body so in that instant I became a monk if only for a spell in my imagination. I have to say it came as a relief. A flood of tears welled up. After Sext the monks eat lunch and have a short siesta.

None at one forty p.m. is the final minor hour before six p.m. Vespers. None with psalms but no Angelus. Hail Mary is said creating a tension that builds towards Compline. Vatican Two abbreviated the liturgy eliminating Prime and seeking as best it could to mitigate Isaac of Stella's torture.

It's all about Mary in the Trappist Abbey. Shaktism pure and simple. As in the Presentation Retreat. What a relief from an Anglican Service all about the man Jesus! All about the Gospel Jesus, the historical even the pseudo-historical Messiah.

Vigil, dreams are set aside at Annunciation of Immaculate Conception. Lauds first light the Virgin sets out to visit the mother of John. Prime early morning the youthful Virgin gives birth to the Messiah. Terce mid-morning the shepherds arrive to see the Christ in the manger but are found staring at Mary. Sext late morning the three Magi arrive from Persia bearing gifts. They at once recognise Mary as Anahita and the Child as Mithras. At None the Virgin brings the Child to the Temple for circumcision, the converse of castration. Certain Cohens proclaim her the Shekinah of the Kabbalah. At Vespers early evening the Holy Family evade capture while Compline first hour of the night the Virgin is Assumed.

> Inherited the woolshed
> Soon got out of sheep
> And classified potatoes on the classing table
> Soon got out of spuds
> The dairy went to beef
> While they should have planted burgundy as far as they were able

Discretion of stirring

You can stay a maximum annual week for your free food and accommodation but I submit that only a retired Christian Brother would do so because there is no orchard, no potager, no brewery, no dairy, no vineyard, no hives. Morale is low. The food on offer is all tinned and packet. A woman comes in from town to cook it. They used to run a dairy herd, sold it in 2000. Now they repackage and dispatch communion wafers.

When the Irish established Notre Dame of Tarrawarra from Mt St Joseph Roscrea at the invitation of Mannix in 1954, they numbered thirty-four souls. Initially, the monks slept together in a dorm where today they have individual bedrooms. In the beginning they communicated through sign language: today they are not unduly taciturn. Back in the day they wore full clobber at all times and in all places: white for novices, black-and-white for choir monks, brown for lay brothers. Today when you wander by their quarters they rock out in civvies.

They were largely men from small Irish holdings, the younger sons of large families, accustomed to rising early in a house with no indoor plumbing and working hard all day with hand-tools in the wind and rain. Family meals were strictly structured, non-negotiable affairs at which the patriarch sat at the head of table and barked orders. There was no TV, no X-box, no time or desire to read and no one left the confines of the farm except to attend Mass or to convey cream to the creamery in a donkey cart. There would have been an occasional piss-up in a pub, a dance at the hall.

When they became Trappists as either lay brothers or choir monks — today all question of subsequent ordination is reserved — they joined a low-tech affair but they didn't give up the grog.

On my third night by happenstance I was the only guest at table as my three fellow guests had checked out that morning. Dom Carthage was rostered on so he served me up my dinner.

I put to him the question.

'Am I too old to become a monk here?'

'Yes. We've geriatrics aplenty. More macaroni?'

'Ta. Can we have a talk?'

'What about?'

'Not about cattle, though about cattle. I thought you were vegetarians. Why would you run beef?'

'Vellum for the scriptorium. More beans?'

'Ta. Did you know I was a prison officer?'

'Is this a confession?'

We all have a tale to tell. Mine focusses on Bourke. Till shortly before Compline, we sit in that beautiful guesthouse dining room with its wainscoted wooden walls, its huge wooden dresser, its open fire that is kept roaring night and day because there's always someone roaming the place to feed and stoke it. Dominus just sat looking in the fire. Once in a while he would sneak a morsel of cold macaroni.

'And so' I concluded 'I would appreciate your view.'

'As I just said to you, the monastery draws and drains the sins of the world. In contemplation a monk draws and drains the sins of the world. But this is about you, I suspect.'

'You don't believe me.'

'I don't know much about stigmata. More of a Capuchin thing. St Francis was stigmatic but so were plenty of hysterics and I recall there's a dervish somewhere can manifest the wounds in battle received by the Most Praised One. Mother Church is rightly suspicious of magic, mate.'

'Magic?'

'Miracles. You don't appear to have enjoyed pastoral support and neither does your Passionist felon, but it's crucial, because Satan can transform himself into an Angel of Light as we read in Two Corinthians. In the late Middle Ages there was so much mysticism, especially among women, the discretion of stirrings and proving of spirits assisted clerics in trying to cope with a multitude of visionaries.'

'So it's a feminine thing?'

'Not entirely. But I have read somewhere strong saints never show stigmata. It sounds like a vision to me but we'd need to determine among the diabolical, the divine, even the digestive.'

'Oh. But the Passionists...'

'I can't speak for the Passionists. It would appear they've already spoken in shutting the book on you, but you can't accept that. I presume they focus on the Passion. We Cistercians are more focussed on the Annunciation. In the twelfth century our mystics had frequent visions of the Holy Child, often as a baby boy on the altar.'

'Good Lord. Sorry. So you're saying it's likely I saw stigmata that weren't actually there?'

'It's possible. It appears to be what the Passionists have concluded, but look: we've a book in our library called *Three Women of Liege*. I suggest you read it. One of these three women could sing complex Latin hymns and chants despite being illiterate. Wonders like these became so commonplace in the late Middle Ages that Austin Friar Walter Hilton actually wrote a treatise for the use of priests engaged in the pastoral care of nuns, warning against the spiritual dangers of seeing and hearing things that others can't. We've a copy of that book as well. It's called *Of Angels' Song*. Are you here tomorrow?'

'I might stick to the books at the top of the stairs. Have you heard of St Isaac of Nineveh?'

'I have. He was Nestorian wasn't he? One of the desert fathers.'

'What exactly does the word 'Nestorian' mean to you? I could never work it out.'

'None is left to tell. Dyophysite maybe. That Mary is not the Mother of God but merely the mother of the man Jesus, first born among many brothers or why would he need to have been baptised?'

'Good point. But you do see my problem, Abba. I can't stop thinking of Simon Bourke. What would you suggest?'

'I say bite the bullet. Ask a suffrage of him. Get it out of the way. Tell him you're in pain. Worth a try. Ask him to clear things up but first, seek the guidance of Holy Church when you get back to where it is you're from.'

'I'm doing that now, aren't I? If you're not Holy Church, who is?'

I have taken from the bookshelf at the top of the stairs a book on St Bernard of SuperMax, an old-fashioned book, the kind you would force on a kid in an old-fashioned school. After Compline Angelus that night I find I cannot sleep so I take up the book and read it at my desk. It certainly puts me away. But just as

I am reaching over to turn off the desk lamp, the book falls open at a certain illustration.

St Bernard is healing a sick man. He is a man of many miracles, St Bernard of Clairvaux. At the dedication of the church at the Abbey of Foigny, he expels a cloud of flies by saying 'Excommunicabe eas'. Next day all the flies are dead and so thick on the pavement they have to be shovelled out.

A sick man is kneeling before the saint. The saint with both hands rested on the man's bent head, like a bishop ordaining a postulant, is muttering something as he raises his own head eyes closed towards Heaven.

Strewth, I thought. If you just change the angle that's exactly what you see as you peek through the judas hole of a slot in which someone is giving the celly a blowie.

I see now why Bourke has been knocked.

> It was what she saw in his eyes I suppose
> As he looked across from his cross
> I can't comment on their love
> Or if whether in Heaven above
> Or some outer circle of Hell
> They persist in it still
> But it's all the comfort I have
> It's all the comfort I need

If credense shuld be gyven to every suche lewd person as wold affirme himself to have revelations from God what redyer way wer ther to subvert al common welths and good orders in the world?

Thomas Cromwell

Proving of spirit

I've had enough. Not taking anything for the pain excepting Panadol. Endless pain of the toothache-in-the-bone variety, cancerous pain. This is no good, I thought. I shall have to go to hospital when I get out of here. I'm going downhill. It'll be a battle to drive home.

I may have exaggerated the volume of shit and spunk in Buzzacott's slot.

Three more guests have now checked in but I don't wish to engage with them so I stay in chapel.

I spend my last two days there. I wasn't sure they mightn't throw me out but they left me where I sat alone at the Notre Dame end with my head in my hands on the foldaway wooden seat in the last stall. I stood as required during the various hours but didn't leave.

It's hard to get your act together when you're on the way out. But for whole blocks of hours at a time I sat there, trying to gain relief. An hour-and-a-half between Vigil and Lauds, an hour-and-a-half between Lauds and Terce, three hours between Terce and Sext, two hours between Sext and None, a full four hours-and-a-half between None and Vespers, an hour-and-a-half between Vespers and Compline. The sun rose and the sun set.

Twenty-eight hours over two full days I sat in that stall, my head in my hands. At the end of Compline on the first day as we filed out in the dark with Dom Carthage sprinkling us with holy water from the green glass font, I fancied I saw him smiling at me and nodding encouragement towards me and thus emboldened I didn't go to bed that night but sat by the fire.

I kept thinking of Brenda. She'd looked so beautiful when she was angry. You should have seen her eyes when she was angry. I realised it was only because I'd loved her we'd stopped having sex. Sex involves perception of difference as well as carnal desire so she'd gone outside the marriage in order to turn back the clock. Understandable, but you do wonder at those marriages in which nothing is resolved and people never feel the need to cleanse the thoughts of their hearts.

To whom did I pray? Ora pro nobis Simon Bourke.

We don't know much about God and I know far too much about Jesus.

Shrive me, holy man.

Can any good thing come out of Goulburn, George Lazenby excepted? I should have to say yes. The Goulburn Church in its death agony coughed up a real Christian.

On the Friday as I checked out I was feeling more secure. I was generous toward the donation box. All my tears in chapel had washed away my pain. After attending a last Terce I drove up to Marysville to see the aftermath of Black Saturday in the Marysville Cemetery, and feeling relieved to be alive and domiciled on Willochra, I booked into a Healesville holiday home I found on the iPhone. There I sat staring at the hills all covered in misty mountain ash while sipping a tasty Tarrawarra Estate pinot noir.

PAX. I keep hearing the words from Terce, you will never die again and reflecting on what I'd read in the *Cistercian Studies Quarterly* concerning Thomas Merton with DT Suzuki, how when you've found the Christ at some point he will disappear like the ox in the Zen ox-herding pictures. Well he'd disappeared for me. And of how, when you have attained peace, you will have nothing left to say and that won't do, will it. Won't do at all.

Next day I was well enough to drive home via Mansfield, lair of Ned Kelly. I found myself turning off the Hume at Yass and heading down the Barton. Before I bid farewell to the koi in the pond where Bob Hawke swam a lap I go through the night without urinating once. That'll do me, I thought. I'm ready. So I drove straight to Shirley's and sat in the ute all night till she came out next morning to walk the dog.

'Dad' she says 'what are you doing here?'
　　'I'm off to see the doctor' I said. 'Would you not come with me, Shirl?'
　　She flexed off and later that day we ventured to Deakin Oncology.

We'd no appointment but Shirley can be very insistent and just to be rid of us I suspect they squeezed me into radiology where I could be given an immediate CT scan as I hadn't eaten. Next day bone scan. Shirley put me up in her spare room and I got to walk the dog by the lake.

Wednesday with Shirley still in tow it is time to learn the results. The oncologist in the Zegna suit is the man who wrote me off back in 2007.

'What's going on here?' he smiles at Shirl.

She doesn't like his tone.

'How's he doing?' she barks.

He raises an eyebrow and leans back in his chair. He won't look at me.

'Not saying it's a miracle,' he says to Shirl, 'but can't find the bugger. Spontaneous regression. Does happen. Just haven't seen it before. You'll have to tell us your secret, Dudley Leahy.'

No I won't. I have learned my lesson there and don't have a lazy half-million euros.

I do have time to think things through.

> O hope of every contrite heart
> O joy of every meek
> To those who fall how kind Thou art
> How good to those who seek!
> While as to those who find, I swear
> No tongue, no pen can show
> The love of Christ: what that may be
> Only His beloved know
> > St Bernard of Clairvaux High Risk Management Correctional Centre

Have a decision and going to the board

Simon Bourke, on the strength of lectio divina, was a contemptuary.

The contemptuary is careful never to resent whatever is said of him and for the sake of his salvation he must commit some act which while neither a crime nor a sin will ensure of his being generally reviled. I saw why the elders always suffered fools
Eleventh-century Sufi Data Ganj Baksh

www.ingramcontent.com/pod-product-compliance
Lightning Source LLC
Chambersburg PA
CBHW031311280626
47169CB00018B/1197